Said and Unsaid
A Coffee and Donuts Book

Amanda Hamm

ISBN: 978-1-943598-99-1

Said and Unsaid is a work of fiction. All names, characters, places, events, etc. are products of the author's imagination or are used fictitiously.

1

*T*he woman only wanted to offer me some pleasant small talk, and all I could think about was the fact that her earrings didn't match.

That's not true.

The earrings matched fine. It was the holes. Whoever pierced Linda's ears had made one hole a teensy bit higher than the other. She'd been sitting with us most Sundays for nearly a year, and I'd never noticed it before. These earrings had three rows each of swinging white beads that seemed to point straight up to the fact that one was hooked closer to the bottom of the earlobe than the other. I suspected she typically wore sets that camouflaged the discrepancy, which meant she was aware of it, which meant she would be embarrassed to know that I noticed, which meant I needed to get out of my head and back into the conversation.

I turned to Joyce as she placed her paper cup of coffee on the table and claimed the seat to my right. "How is everyone this morning?" she asked. I'm not sure if it was Joyce or the hard folding chair that groaned as her weight settled into it.

"No news yet," Linda said.

"Maybe you're wrong." Maria smiled up at her husband, Antonio, who had arrived at the table with two cups. He placed one in front of her before he sat down with the other. We were complete now. Six cups of coffee and zero donuts.

"No," Linda said, "this isn't wishful thinking. She's definitely acting suspicious. And David gave her a significant look the other day." She nodded knowingly. She'd told us two weeks ago that she was convinced her daughter was pregnant and not telling anyone yet.

"I hope you're right," Joyce said. "Grandkids bring such joy to life. Of course you know I'm starting to look towards the great-grands. Maybe Alexa will help." She nudged my shoulder playfully. She'd been threatening to introduce me to her grandson forever.

Since it hadn't happened yet, I assumed he wasn't interested in being fixed up. I smiled and sipped my coffee as I hoped it was his loss and not mine.

"Oh, I doubt our young friend has any trouble meeting men on her own." That was Suzy. She was my most embarrassing ally. Every week she found a way to insinuate that men flocked to me and every week she asked if I had met anyone new and every week I was forced to admit that I was still as single as I had been the last three years. She tucked a section of her gray-blond bob behind her ear before she waved the same magenta-manicured finger in my direction. "Look at those lovely dark eyes and lashes," she said. "How many young men did you have to fight off this week?"

"None," I said. *And I'm not sure I'd put up a fight anyway.*

She smiled slyly. "Oh, you're a private one. We'll know when you finally meet a man who floats your boat though."

"We'll see it on her face for sure," Linda added with an annoyingly smug nod.

"Our oldest is coming home for a visit next week." Maria told me with a sympathetic glance that she was changing the subject on purpose. She and Antonio were closest to my age of anyone at the table, and the daughter she spoke of was only a year younger than me. I already stuck out as an oddball. That's why I never got a donut.

Sacred Heart served coffee and donuts between the two Sunday masses as a way for parishioners to socialize. People of all ages sat at scattered tables amid running children, most of them enjoying donuts. The donut line had shortened now, but no one else at my table ever had a donut. If I was going to be the only one under thirty and the only one under forty, then I didn't need to also be the only one stuffing my face.

"That's nice," Linda said to Maria. "How long is she staying?" Her earlobes still didn't match, but with her head turned that way I only saw one and it wasn't bothering me.

"Only a few days."

"Will that include Sunday?" The magenta fingers were holding a coffee cup halfway to Suzy's mouth.

"Not this time."

"The poor child with be deprived of one of my excellent homilies." Monsignor Loy had walked up to our table. He had one hand over his heart as though he keenly felt the loss on her behalf.

"That would be sad indeed," Maria said. "But I think we'll be attending on Saturday… before she leaves."

"Perfect," he said, bouncing on his heels. The man was probably in his fifties and had a balding head and a long white beard. The first Sunday I came to Sacred Heart was Pentecost, and the red vestments gave him a skinny sort of Victorian Santa Claus vibe. His eyes landed on me with some concern. "How are you, my sheep?"

It sounded like a casual question, but I had visited him a few times recently for something like counseling that I refused to think of as counseling. I knew he was giving me a chance to let him know if I needed another appointment. "I'm pretty good, thank you." *Pray for me, but not if it makes you worry.*

He nodded and I think he heard what I didn't say. Then he looked at Linda. "And you?"

She laughed. "Don't spend any time fretting over me."

"I will see where else I am needed then. Enjoy your coffee." Monsignor Loy moved to another table, and we continued our chat until my coffee was gone.

"All right, everyone," I said as I stood. "I need to take care of Paws. I'll see you next week." I tossed my cup in the trash on my way out of the parish hall. The sun was bright and warm on a beautiful summer day. I lived in an apartment complex next door to the church so I came on foot most Sundays. A dog park where I would soon end up was right across the street. I had to drive more than ten miles each way for work but on most weekends, this little corner of Thompsonville was my world.

I walked up the steps to my second floor apartment. The numbers one, zero, two and four spelled out my address on the door and the four was my nemesis. It was different than the others. They were all black metal, but the four was smaller and had a slantier font, as though someone italicized my address but missed three numbers. It drew my attention every single time I came to the door and I was sick of looking at it.

When I unlocked and opened the door, Paws stood up in her crate and began wagging her tail violently. She was a lap-dog-sized mutt with black and white speckled fur and mostly black paws. She had expressive ears that sometimes stuck up and sometimes lay back on her head. It was nice to have someone uncomplicated to welcome me home.

"Hey, girl," I said. "Did you miss me?"

I opened her crate and she ran around my legs like a cat before she bounded into my bedroom. She knew my habits as well as I did.

I took off the dress I'd worn to church and hung it in my closet before I picked out casual summer clothes. My dark hair was mostly straight, but it curled at the ends and I thought it made a cute ponytail, starting at the crown of my head and bouncing off my neck when I walked.

"Almost ready," I said to Paws. "Just going to check my phone." I found that I had missed a call from my dad. I slipped the phone into my pocket. I'd call him later. He was probably calling to find out why I was not talking to my mom.

That's not true.

I wasn't *not talking* to her. I was only taking a break from talking to her. It was true that she didn't understand the difference, but I hoped I was doing the right thing.

When I picked up the leash, Paws sat without being told and waited for me to hook it to her collar. Then she flung herself into the air a few times as we headed out the door.

There wasn't much traffic on the street we had to cross. I still took Paws the extra twenty feet or so to the crosswalk. If we were out to get some exercise it seemed silly to avoid steps. I saw a few familiar faces at the dog park and a few familiar dogs. I knew the names of the dogs because they were regularly called out. The people's names I didn't know. The dog park was the one place I never tried to make friends. I was there for Paws, who was my one true friend. I let her go to play with the other dogs, and I picked a spot in a corner where I could observe and enjoy a little quiet. I was kind of small-talked out for the day anyway.

After a few minutes, I noticed a guy in a white baseball hat who seemed to be making his way towards me. I thought I might have seen him before but not enough to know which dog was his. He was making his way towards me with his eyes on the dogs, but the path was too straight not to be intentional. He took a couple decisive steps as he faced me and said, "Hi."

"Hi," I said. *I don't like baseball hats.*

"Which dog is yours?" he asked.

"The white and black one," I said, pointing at Paws. *That's why she's running laps around me.*

"How long have you had him? Or her?"

"Her," I said. "About three years."

"This is a nice park." He turned to survey the area. He looked back at me with an expression that flipped between apology and desperation. It seemed he was picking up on the fact that I wanted him to go away. I felt guilty. I shouldn't be rude just because I was trying to figure out how my dad and I could talk about my mom without really talking about anything. This guy didn't care about my problems.

"Which dog is yours?" I asked. I wasn't entirely faking the interest.

"I, uh…" He gestured to a dog sniffing a nearby tree. "I brought the dachshund. Her name is Baby, but I didn't name her."

He fidgeted with mild embarrassment. I assumed that if he didn't name the dog that meant he had rescued her from a shelter that already named her. In my book, that was nothing to be ashamed of. I hadn't named Paws either. "She's cute," I said. "Have you brought her here before?"

He shook his head. "I'm sort of new to the area. Um… Tracker Briggs." He held his hand out to me.

I took it briefly and said, "Alexa. How new is sort of new?"

"Well, I grew up here, but I was away for school and just moved back."

"What were you studying?"

"Analytics. I just finished my Master's and now I'm working at an insurance place. It's, um, I guess I like it so far."

"That's good. I mean that you like it. You wouldn't want all those years of school to go to waste." I smiled to show that I was mostly teasing. It sounded like a boring job to me but probably no more so than my own.

He returned the smile cautiously. "You sound like my mom."

"Is that a good thing?"

He shrugged and stuffed his hands into his pockets. The toe of his shoe kicked at a rock and drew both of our attention. In the silence that followed, I let my eyes return to his face slowly. The calves sticking out of his shorts were muscular but hairy. He was very thin and his hands were larger than mine. I'd detected that at the handshake. They weren't beefy at all, just had long fingers. I noticed that his bottom lip was unusually fuller than the top which for some odd reason put thoughts in my head that should not be there in the presence of a stranger. I wanted to take a closer look at his eyes, but I really did not like baseball hats. I scanned the park for Paws as I made the brilliant remark that, "I like this weather."

I caught a nod out of the corner of my eye before he asked, "Are you here only on Sundays?"

"No, I bring Paws after work almost any day it isn't wet. We can't come if it's wet because she likes to roll in the mud."

"Sounds like harmless fun," he said with a laugh.

"It might be if she didn't hate baths so much."

His eyes widened. "She's not a biter, is she?"

"Oh, no. She just sort of curls in on herself all pathetically and looks at me like it's my fault."

"Has it ever been your fault?"

I could tell he was kidding, but I didn't know exactly what he meant so I laughed and tried to give him a puzzled look at the same time.

He shrugged and seemed to be rolling his eyes at himself. "I have no clue what I'm talking about."

For some reason, that made it funnier to me. I stopped laughing when I realized he had turned a bit red.

"I should probably go," he said.

"All right. It was nice to meet you." I tried not to sound disappointed or relieved as he waved with one hand and pulled a leash from his pocket with the other. Though I might have been disappointed *and* relieved. I didn't want him to go because of anything I had said or laughed at. Something about him was making me tense though, making me wish I could run after Paws.

I watched him scoop up the little dachshund and clip a leash to her before putting her back on the ground. She folded her legs and refused to walk. He picked her up again, and I was still watching him when he turned back and smiled at me. A brief heady feeling made me glad I'd opened myself up for a friendly conversation.

The weather really could not have been more perfect so it wasn't only a desire to delay a certain phone call that made me spend another hour at the park, alternating between reading a book on my phone and watching Paws run around with a stick in her mouth.

2

*I*n some ways my relationship with my dad was simpler than the one with my mom or with my sister. We rarely talked about anything serious, which meant we rarely had anything to argue about. I was nine when he moved out. I spent a few years pretending to be thrilled every time I saw him while simmering anger burned on the inside, waiting for him to notice my act. Until I realized that he didn't care if I was acting. From that point we had a distant but cordial relationship. He paid for me to go to college. He didn't come to watch me graduate. In some ways the relationship was not so simple.

We were generally able to get along so I wasn't worried that he was going to yell at me about the thing with Mom. I was uncomfortable talking about it because I wasn't sure I was doing the right thing. She was already so upset about Megan, and I didn't want to be like my sister.

I had a quick lunch then sat down with my phone. This was when I normally called my mom. That made it even more strange to dial my dad.

"Alexa?" he said as he answered. He actually sounded as though there was a chance someone else would call from my phone.

"Hi, Dad. Um... how are you?"

"Fine, honey. I'm out golfing today. Is the sky this blue where you are?"

"I'm glad you're enjoying it. I won't keep you long. I just wondered if you called me this morning for a reason."

"Yeah, I... well, I ran into your mom."

By ran into, I was sure he meant she had stopped in his office to talk.

"She, uh… she thinks you've also decided to cut her out of your life. That's not really what's going on, is it?"

"Nothing so dramatic." I sighed and reached my free hand down to pat Paws. Soft fur was a good stress reliever. "I just felt we needed a break. I told her I was going to skip a Sunday call or two while I… while I thought about some things." *I'm praying about it, but you know I can't say that.* It was too close to the one major exception to me getting along with my dad. When I was twenty years old, he found out that I had become a Christian and we had a huge yelling contest that neither of us had ever mentioned again, not even to apologize.

"So you're not, like, giving her the silent treatment or anything?" He sounded uncomfortable and I knew he was asking me only to avoid talking about it with my mom again.

"No, Dad. I'm really not trying to be juvenile here. I just… We've been fighting, and I want a little peace while I figure out what I'm doing wrong."

"All right, honey. I should get back to my game. Is that God thing still working out for you?"

"Yeah. Bye, Dad."

He asked some version of that last question every time we talked. I honestly couldn't tell if he was being snide or if it was his way of acknowledging that his opinions weren't going to change my beliefs. I only ever said yeah or fine or something else benign in response because I feared a more thorough answer would be a case of poking the bear.

Megan's name was next to my dad's in the contact list because they had the same last name. That was the only reason I even considered calling my sister next. I knew it would be fruitless at best though. On the incredibly slim chance she actually answered, we'd be fighting in twenty-five words or less.

Megan was about a year and a half older than me. Because of where our birthdays fell and the fact that she did first grade twice, we ended up going through most of school in the same grade. She resented having her little sister in her class, and it was a constant source of friction between us.

Soon after we began high school, Megan gained a reputation that made her popular with certain guys and I spent four years actively avoiding any similar associations. I entered college having never been on a single date because I was desperate to keep people from talking about me. The irony of course was that they talked about my inexperience as much as they talked about Megan's experience.

She didn't graduate with me. She dropped out at the beginning of our senior year, and it took Mom two years to convince her to get a GED. She changed jobs every few months since and had been arrested twice for DUI. I lived about two hours from the rest of my family and that had been a calculated move. I called Mom most Sundays to check in. She always managed to bring the conversation to my sister.

I tried to hold my tongue and just listen. I hoped if I kept quiet we could move on to a new topic. Mom would goad me though. She'd take my silence as confirmation that her terrible mothering was responsible for Megan's problems and then she'd become irate. Or I'd try to calm her down and end up agitated myself. We could not talk about Megan without fighting, and Mom couldn't talk about anything else.

My dog had curled into a ball at my feet while I mulled the less-than-healthy dynamics of my family. "Come on, girl," I called to her as I moved to my living room sofa. She jumped next to me and put her head in my lap. I dug my fingers into the soft fur around her ears. "You're my witness," I said. "I'm going to sit here and pray about this. Monsignor Loy agreed that taking a break isn't necessarily avoidance. It might be the way to break this pattern."

I sighed with a small touch of contentment as I closed my eyes. I loved the way Paws looked at me. She looked as though everything I said was brilliant. And that made me feel a little better.

~~~~

I had three bosses. Three men who expected me to type things and send emails and schedule appointments and fill databases and throw an occasional office party. It wasn't difficult to juggle because they all seemed to think the other two were demanding more of me than they were. And they were all fairly nice. I generally liked my job. I always liked coming home better though.

Paws was waiting for me as soon as I unlocked my eyes from the still warped number four that marked and marred my apartment. I changed out of my work clothes into shorts again so we could visit the dog park before I made myself dinner. I stood in front of the mirror a few moments longer than usual trying to decide if the ponytail was cute enough.

Then I asked myself why I was trying to impress a bunch of dogs anyway. I looked down at Paws. "I'm not thinking what you think I'm thinking."

She ran in a quick circle that I decided to interpret as her not contradicting me.

"All right, let's go." I waved her towards the front door where I picked up her leash.

We were at the park in minutes. It felt more like summer, and I was glad I had pulled my hair up so it wasn't sticking to the back of my neck. It was less crowded than the weekend. With fewer canine buddies for her, I ran back and forth with Paws a while to make sure she was moving around. Then I tossed a stick, which she refused to bring back. I was watching her run around with it when I noticed the dachshund sitting nearby.

I looked over to see the same guy as yesterday in different clothes but the same white baseball hat. "Hello again," he said.

"Hi. Baby talked you into coming back, huh?"

He smiled. "She made some good arguments."

Paws ran by with her stick. "I'm not going to chase you," I said to her. "That's not how fetch works."

"I didn't realize you had to teach dogs fetch. Isn't that supposed to be an instinct?"

I shrugged. Paws was the only dog I'd owned. I didn't know if she was the exception or the rule.

"So, uh… you remembered the dog's name. Do you remember mine?"

Uh, oh. "I do." I made a fake grab for the stick as Paws ran by again to tease her and to cover – I hoped – that I didn't prove I remembered his name.

He wore a playful expression when I turned back to him. He said, "Are you telling me the truth, Alexa?"

Oh, no. He used my name which forced me to think of his and forced me to think the thing I'd been trying not to think since he first told me it. The guy had a dog's name. Maybe I only thought that because of where we were, but I thought it and now it was in my head and I could never say his name out loud because he would hear it in my voice. He would hear me thinking *you have a dog's name.*

I was sure all those thoughts ran through my head in less than a second, but it must have been longer because Tracker started laughing. I was pretty sure he was laughing at me. "Nice filter," he said.

"What do you mean?" Come on. Surely I could muster more innocence than that.

"I appreciate you holding back," he said. "It's amazing how many people ask me if Tracker is a nickname – or just assume it is – without realizing that it sounds like they're saying, 'Hey, were your parents on something when they named you?'"

His attitude helped me relax and so did the fact that I was being honest when I said, "I promise it never occurred to me that it might not be your real name." *Only that you might have been named after a dog.*

"I *want* to believe you." He met my eye only a second before he looked away. Then he sucked in a quick breath and said, "I think this is after work for you, right? Where do you work?"

"Thompsonville Credit Union. I do secretary stuff."

"How long have you worked there?"

"Almost three years. I think I like it."

"You answered two questions in one. Am I that predictable?" He smiled as though he was kidding, but the opposite of confidence veiled his face.

"Maybe I'm better at reading your mind." *Which would be wonderful because I am still thinking that I am talking to a guy with a dog's name.*

"I hope not." It may not have been the sun that tinted his face red. "I… um… I'm doing some math here. You said you had your dog three years and you had your job three years and I'm going to guess that's either how long you've been out of school or how long you've lived in Thompsonville. Am I close?"

"Yes. On both counts. I moved here the summer after I graduated. It was only a four-year degree so I'm not as scholarly as some people." *I was paying attention to everything you said last time, even if I couldn't prove I remembered your name.* "And I adopted Paws right away. I did a few things through a temp agency until the credit union job became permanent so that's why I said almost three years."

"I think there are two branches of the credit union. Do you work at the one on Townline Street or Miller Bend?"

Townline. Am I paranoid not to want to tell you where I work? "There are three branches actually."

"Where's the third one?"

"It's in the Havens Creek shopping center."

"I'm not surprised I didn't know that. Is that the one where you work?"

I tried to look coy and not defensive. "Maybe."

"Am I asking too many questions?" Tracker said. "You didn't come here to be interrogated, did you?" He waved his hand towards the three other people in the park – all of them staring at phones – as though they were examples of what I'd prefer.

I wanted to tell Tracker that I'd much rather be talking to him than staring at my phone. I didn't want to give him the wrong idea though. He could probably tell I was enjoying myself anyway because I was laughing at him again. "You do know you just asked me two more questions, right?"

"Man, I am so annoying." He picked up his hat with one hand and shoved the other hand through his hair before he slammed the hat back down. I didn't get a good look, but I was fairly sure he wasn't covering early balding. "Maybe I should leave you alone and just play with the dog for a while," he said.

We both looked at Baby. She was stretched out in a shady spot and appeared reluctant to move. A doubtful expression clouded Tracker's face. He turned his attention to Paws, who was still running around with the same stick, and he said, "Can I chase her if you're not going to?"

"I guess."

He crouched and held out his hand as though he was asking her for the stick. She jumped into a play bow, daring him to come and get it. He made a move towards her and the dog flinched but stayed where she was. Then he actually started running and Paws took off. I watched him chase her around a tree, and Paws kept looking over her shoulder to see that he was still coming after her. Baby was the only one who didn't seem interested in the game. She might have been trying to sleep. I wondered if she and Tracker were mismatched.

I could tell that Tracker wasn't trying very hard to catch Paws. And then I discovered that my dog is kind of stupid. Tracker picked up a different stick and waved it triumphantly at her. Paws dropped the stick she had and ran towards him. He jogged back to me with my dog on his heels. Tracker handed me the stick with a goofy flourish. "I won this for you," he said.

Paws sat in front of us, and I swear her ears were cocked in a way that said she wanted me to explain how she'd been bested. "Did you have fun?" I asked.

"Yes." Tracker grinned at me. "I know you were talking to the dog."

"I'm glad you both had fun."

"Well, I think Baby was done as soon as we got here so I should take her home."

"Okay." *Please come back tomorrow.*

He pulled a phone from the pocket on the front of his shorts and put it back without looking at it. Then he took a leash from the other pocket. "So I guess we'll go and, um… maybe we'll see you again unless… well…" He unfolded the leash then bunched it up again. "We'll go now."

Baby required a bit of encouragement to leave the park. Once she was moving, she trotted behind Tracker happily enough. He waved to me as he closed the gate behind them. I waved back and then squatted in front of Paws. I clipped the leash to her and said, "You like him, don't you?"

Her ears came together as though pushed up by a doggy smile.

"Don't get your hopes up," I warned her. "We barely know him."

She just kept looking excited. Stupid dog. Why was this the only time she didn't seem to see the wisdom of my words?

3

*N*othing interesting happened the next day.

That's not true.

We got some rain, and I suppose that was interesting. The park was too wet and therefore muddy on Tuesday for me to take Paws. We had to settle for walking along a dry sidewalk instead.

That was the only reason I let her stay extra time at the park the next day. We were not waiting for anyone in particular to show up or hoping for anyone in particular to show up. I mean, she's a *dog*. She didn't care if she was wrestling a stick from another mutt or a pug or a dachshund or whatever. Neither of us cared a bit who was or was not there. I was simply letting her make up for the time she missed the previous day.

Of course we stayed at the park so long I was almost late for my class at the gym. I was doing cycling on Wednesday nights. I joined the class in an effort to make some friends and it was going very well. I don't think anyone there – not even the instructors – remembered my name, and the only person I'd been talking to at all hadn't been there the last few weeks. She may have moved for all I knew.

I still enjoyed having a bit of exercise that did not involve picking up poop.

I came into the room just as the music started, loud music with bass that made my ribs vibrate. I sat on the first empty cycle I saw and pedaled lightly as the instructor guided us through a warm-up. An older woman wearing a purple sweatband across her forehead took the cycle next to me a few minutes into the class. She was wearing earbuds and made no eye contact.

Earbuds. That was what I spent most classes puzzling over.

Probably a quarter of the people in the room had them in their ears each week, and I just couldn't figure it out. The music in the room was so loud I was pretty sure you'd have to blow out your eardrums to overpower it with a different playlist. The instructor used a microphone and was still a challenge to understand because the music was that loud.

I wondered if perhaps silent earbuds were an attempt to muffle the speakers surrounding us. Even so, it didn't answer my larger question. Was it rude? Was it rude to be in a class making what looked like an obvious attempt to ignore the instructor? This wasn't school. Maybe it was okay to do your own thing on the bikes. I just wished I could stop thinking about it. Was it rude to wear earbuds if it made some crazy person next to you ask worthless questions in her head?

After class, I tried to talk to the woman in the purple sweatband as she pulled her earbuds out. "Hi," I said. "Good class today?"

She half shrugged and half nodded.

"I'm here every Wednesday. This might be my favorite instructor." *Like it matters when they all say the same things, but this guy's voice isn't annoying.*

"He's all right," she said.

"Do your legs feel like jelly, too?"

"I'm used to it." She walked away as though proving her legs were fine.

I'm sorry for bothering you. How do I know who wants to talk without trying?

After dinner that night I decided to call my mom. It was Wednesday and not Sunday. That was the most concrete thing I'd come up with to start fresh. I intended to make it a very quick call and not give either of us time to start yelling.

She didn't answer. That probably meant she was now not talking to me because I was not talking to her even though I *wasn't* not talking to her. I was pretty much expecting voicemail though. "Hi, Mom. It's me. I'm sorry if I hurt your feelings last time we talked. I just called to say hi. I'll try to touch base with you again soon."

Encouraged by the simplicity of one-sided conversation and maybe some other unexplained whim, I sent Megan a brief text.

It said: `Hi, sis.  Hope you're good.`

Already in my pajamas, I curled up on the sofa with Paws and a book. My phone surprised me with a buzz before I found my page. I jumped back up and Paws kept the seat warm while I read my sister's reply. It said: `Back at you.`

I stared at it for a moment. Megan just texted me. I could hardly believe it. This was huge. I put the phone down, sensing rather than knowing that I should leave well enough alone for now. Megan and I would never be best buddies. We were too different. I had accepted that. I only wanted us to forgive each other for things we'd said and done as kids and teenagers and get along as adults. There could be peace between any two people who both wanted it. I wasn't trying for friendship with her, only peace. This was the first moment I dared to hope that she wanted peace, too.

Paws lifted her head as I sat so she could slip it back into my lap. I ruffled her fur. "I think maybe this was a good day," I told her. She accepted the point with a sigh that was almost a doggy purr.

~~~~

One of my bosses was sick on Thursday and a nutty woman who worked with me spent half the day disinfecting all the phones and light switches and anything else she could get her handy wipes on. I called her nutty – in a non-offensive way – right to her face because the man who was sick had the sense to stay home with his germs.

Someone had taken my parking space when I got home. We didn't have assigned spaces, but that one was mine because I parked there every day and I was pretty sure that made it mine. I felt guilty about taking the space to the left because I was pretty sure someone else had perceived ownership over that space and I just knew I was setting in motion a whole, horrible domino thing for the rest of the evening.

I walked up the stairs and faced down the one, the zero, the two and the *four* as I wondered for the five-thousandth time how anyone could think it was acceptable to fix my address with mismatched numbers. Paws was already standing in her crate when I opened the door, her tail smacking against the side of it.

"Hi, girl," I said. I put down my bag and went to let her out. "Did you miss me?"

She pushed her head against my hand as though there was any chance I'd forget to pet her. Then she ran ahead of me to the bedroom, continuing her show of thinking she might be in charge.

I pulled two shirts out of my drawer and held them up. "Blue or green?"

Paws yipped in agreement.

"This is why you need me," I told her. "You can't be in charge if you don't even know a question when you hear one."

Paws nodded at me.

That's not true.

She sneezed. But it sure looked like she nodded at me.

Once I was comfortable, I took Paws outside. I was locking my door when the one across the hall opened.

"Alexa!"

I don't think she meant to shout at me, but my neighbor had one of those voices that didn't seem to have a volume control. I always knew when she had friends over because her cackling laugh would seep through the hallway into my apartment like snow getting under a glove.

I turned and said, "Hi, Deborah." I knew three things about this woman. Her first name, which clearly was Deborah. Her appearance, which always included massive bags under her eyes and colorful scrubs. And that she owned a dog, which was the only reason she ever talked to me.

"Could you be a dear and take Sampson with you today?" Deborah said. "I would owe you big time."

Sincerity would be enough. "Yeah. I'll take him."

"One second." Deborah reached into her apartment and produced a leash. She handed me one end. Sampson was already tethered to the other end. "You're a lifesaver," she said with an exaggerated sigh.

Sampson was tugging on the leash in his hurry to get to the stairs. I acknowledged Deborah's showy gratitude with a nod and made my way to the grass with a dog attached to each arm. Both animals lunged for the green to relieve themselves. "All right, guys," I said to them. "Now we might have a problem."

Sampson was a yellow dog who I guessed was some sort of Lab mix, though he was smaller than most Labs. He wasn't a problem by himself. He was a friendly dog and he and Paws didn't seem to mind each other. But I couldn't let him off leash. He wouldn't come when I called him, and I'd found out the hard way that he would try to slip out the gate at the park while others were coming or going. I could still go to the park and just keep Sampson tied up. That felt a little unfair though.

"Let's just head that way and see what the park looks like today." I gave both leashes a gentle nudge forward. We crossed the street and I guided Paws away from the gate, planning to walk the length of the park first. Maybe we could do a short walk, take Sampson home, and then come back.

The park was not crowded. I only saw two people. One of them was crouched down with his back to me. He was wearing a white baseball hat and petting a long-haired dachshund. I still didn't like the hat, but my stomach didn't know that because it was trying to jolt electricity into me at the sight.

The guy turned as he stood, and he waved happily when he saw me. I wiggled my hands to show that I didn't have one free to wave. Tracker jogged up to the fence, and I stopped to wait for him. Because that was polite.

"Hey, Alexa. You're not coming in today?"

"I'm sort of babysitting." I gestured to Sampson. "This one's not good off leash so I thought we'd just walk." *Maybe. Or maybe we could come back. Or maybe I'll go ahead and be unfair to Sampson if you suggest it. Please suggest I come in.*

"Can I... would you mind if I come out and walk with you?"

That might work, too. "We'll wait," I said. I stood there and watched him grab Baby and carry her around to the outside of the fence. He set her on the sidewalk and secured her leash while I let myself think the scary question. Was he only being friendly or was Tracker Briggs... was he interested in me?

He smiled at me as we started moving. "So tell me about the extra dog."

"That's Sampson. He belongs to my neighbor. I'm just walking him for her."

"Do you, um... never mind."

"Do I what?"

I was watching the dogs and caught a sheepish shrug out of the corner of my eye. "I was going to ask if you walk him a lot, but I'm trying not to be a pest and that doesn't seem like a good start."

"I probably walk him a couple times a month, although it seems to be becoming more frequent," I said. "It's not a big deal when I'm coming out with Paws anyway."

We were both quiet a minute before Tracker nodded towards Sacred Heart as we passed it. "That's my church," he said.

I smiled teasingly. "You own it?"

"I go there." He clarified with fake annoyance.

At least I hoped it was fake. "Me, too," I said.

He nodded. "You a cradle Catholic?"

"No, I…" This was embarrassing to admit. "I sort of converted by accident."

"By accident?" There was laughter in his voice. "That sounds like a story. Is it one you mind telling?"

That was a thorny question. It was a story with two parts, and I had never told anyone the first part. I went to a party my first year of college. It was only a few weeks into the school year and I had already developed a crush on a guy in one of my classes. He invited me to the party. I naively thought it was going to be my first date.

I looked for the guy when I arrived at the house. He told me he was glad I'd come and he handed me a cup of something he called punch. He walked away as he told me to go enjoy myself. I stayed close enough that I heard him telling a few other kids – boys and girls – that he was glad they came. I tried not to be hurt that I wasn't singled out for an invitation and to make the best of the situation.

One sip told me it was a bad idea to drink what was in my cup. When I thought no one was looking, I dumped half of it into a houseplant that might have been plastic. I thought people would think I was drinking but with some left in the cup they wouldn't offer me more. The music was too loud to exchange more than choppy sentences with people a foot away, and I was thinking of leaving when I caught a glimpse of the guy I knew at the edge of the room. He waved me over to join him.

I had to make my way through a crowd. When I got to the spot I had seen him, a hand grabbed my arm and pulled me into a separate room. The door closed and the music dulled but didn't quiet. I realized two things that made my heart beat just as loudly in my ears. The first was that the guy holding my arm – he was still holding my arm – was a person I had never seen before. He only looked like the guy from my class from a distance because they were wearing the same red baseball hat. The other thing I noticed was that we were alone in a small bedroom.

He lunged at me and put his mouth on mine. I pushed at him and told him I didn't even know his name. He told me his name and kissed me again, this time with his free hand trying to bring my body closer to his. The taste of alcohol on his breath turned my stomach as I struggled to break away from him. He let me take a step back, but his hand still gripped my forearm. I tried to get him to let go. He laughed like we were playing a game even though I was crying.

"You need another drink," he said.

I didn't have time to argue before the door popped open behind him. A couple staggered into the room and burst into hysterical laughter at finding it "taken." The guy released me, and I used the distraction to flee not only the room but the whole house. I ran all the way back to my dorm.

A few weeks later that same guy in my class mentioned a Bible study on campus. He wasn't talking to me and I didn't care because I had cooled on him considerably. But I overheard him telling a fellow classmate about the group. His tone suggested the Bible study was the exact opposite of the party and that's what got my attention. And that was the part of the story I could tell Tracker Briggs.

"I heard about a Bible study when I was in college," I said. "I was a freshman and it sounded like a place I could meet some nice people and maybe make a few friends. I went even though I... well, my dad is an atheist. He and my mom got divorced when I was little and she was raised in the Methodist church so she took me and my sister sporadically after he left but we never really... It wasn't really part of our lives. The others in the group didn't mind. Actually they got all excited like they were going to be saving me, you know?"

Tracker smiled as though he could picture that.

"They were mostly nice people so I kept going even though I secretly scoffed at it changing my life in any way. I even started going to church with them as, like, a social thing. And then sometime in my sophomore year it dawned on me that I had gotten into the habit of praying and that I must believe there was someone on the other end or else... why else would I pray?"

I thought it was something I could share with the guy I met this week, but I felt self-conscious as soon as the words were out of my mouth. What if he'd been expecting something more profound? Did I make it sound insignificant? This was only supposed to be a casual conversation after all. I shifted the leashes in my hands and pretended the effort was distracting me from expecting a reaction.

"I think I had an experience that was similar," Tracker said. "I mean, it was similar and completely different."

I swallowed whatever retort I had about how little sense that made. If he wasn't going to laugh at me then I wasn't going to laugh at him. "Can you explain that?"

"I can't believe you don't know exactly what I meant." Apparently, laughing at himself was fair game. "I was raised in the church. There was a priest who said something... It was the one before Monsignor Loy and he wasn't really talking to me. Or not just to me. He was talking to a whole room full of teenagers and he said something like, 'At some point you need to believe in God because you actually believe and not because your parents tell you that you do.' At first, it really shook me up. I was like, 'What if I don't?' or 'What if I can't really believe?' and I spent a lot of time thinking about it. Obsessing about it really. But eventually I figured out that all my thinking and worrying boiled down to me asking God whether or not I believed in him."

It made perfect sense, and it made me laugh.

Tracker eyed me as though he wanted to be sure we were laughing at the same thing.

"It struck me as funny that I would also call that similar yet completely different."

He smiled and bumped my arm with his elbow. "You doubted the wisdom of my comparison?"

I never liked roller coasters, that feeling that my stomach had just jumped outside my body. There was a similar yet completely different sensation when Tracker touched me, and for once I didn't hate it. I still kind of wanted to run away though. I kept walking as though I was perfectly calm. I walked as though the stretching silence wasn't awkward for me.

"You got something unexpected out of that Bible study," he said. "But did you find the friends you were looking for?"

Ouch. Another question with thorns. The two people I'd been closest to were guys I dated. Separately of course. They both dumped me. Also separately. Two very separate, very painful events. "Yeah," I said. "Sort of. I spent most of my time with one girl who moved farther away than I did after graduation. We really only keep in touch online anymore."

"That's too bad." He paused then proved he was paying too much attention to what I was saying. "You said you went to church with your mom and your sister. You just have the one sister then?"

Was it my fault or his that all of his questions were poking me uncomfortably? I said, "Yes," for simplicity's sake even if it wasn't the entire truth. "Let's talk about you now." I was tired of dodging.

"Okay," he said. "What do you want to know?"

"Hmm…" *Are you single? Are you going to ask me out? Will you eventually break my heart? How do you feel about having a dog's name?* Maybe asking the questions wasn't any easier. "I don't know," I said. "Just tell me something interesting."

"Oh. Pressure." He winced and looked thoughtful. "I used to be a drummer."

"Really? Care to elaborate?"

"I played in high school. Yes, marching band and everything. Then in college a couple of guys asked if I'd help them put together a band. We were more like a basement band than a garage band so it was, you know… much cooler." He flashed me a grin. It was like a wink without a wink. "We played together for several months at least but then this one guy got all pushy about 'Let's get a gig' and 'We gotta play in front of people' and I was like 'Can we just have fun without embarrassing ourselves?' Eventually there was enough friction that I quit. I don't know if they ever got another drummer."

"What if they did and went and got famous without you?"

"I wouldn't care."

I believed him.

"But I'm 99% sure they're not famous."

Were we getting on well enough for good-natured ribbing? I tried, "So you're saying you guys sucked?"

"No." He kept a straight face but showed me the smile in his eyes. I finally looked close enough to tell that they were blue. Maybe I liked blue eyes more than I disliked baseball hats. "There's a big difference between sucking and professional musicians," he said. "I like to think we were somewhere in the vicinity of okay. But we didn't have a name anyway. You can't be famous without a good name."

"Maybe they found a new drummer who was better than you, *and* better at coming up with names than you."

"Not possible." Tracker pulled himself up to walk a little taller. "I actually had a very awesome band name that I never told the others because I didn't want to waste it."

"What is it?"

"I'm not telling."

"Why not?"

"Well, I don't know you very well. What if you're the kind of person who goes around stealing band names?"

I sighed at him, the kind of sigh intended to be heard. "You are so full of it," I said. "You have no brilliant band name."

"Ha. I'm not falling for that. You're just trying to trick me into revealing the name."

"All right. Tell me something else then."

"About me?"

I shrugged, trying to back off some of the enthusiasm I showed by mistake. I didn't know him very well either.

"I, uh... I have six nieces and nephews, and I'm the godfather of two of them." There was pride in his voice and... Was that joy? I wanted to know a guy who could speak of his family with joy.

"Six?" I said. "How many siblings did that take?"

"I have four older sisters." He studied me for a moment. "It's funny. Usually when I tell that to another guy, I get a look of utter sympathy. And when I tell girls I see a reaction that looks like 'And you probably deserved everything they ever did to you.' But you don't..." He smiled thoughtfully then looked away, almost certainly because he could tell I was squirming inside.

"So anyway," he said. "Four sisters. Right now one has no kids, one has one kid, one just had a second, and one has three. Not in age order. It's the second oldest who doesn't have kids and the one closest to me who has two and... They're all married and live pretty close. The one who lives farthest is not quite an hour's drive. Mom and Dad were something like thrilled when I decided to move back here and complete the unit. That's what Mom said. She tries to get us all together whenever anyone has a birthday or a milestone or if it's, like, Flag Day or something." He was laughing and rolling his eyes at what sounded like a nice big family.

A big *happy* family. I was so jealous it hurt. Too much. It hurt too much because I thought Tracker could see it. He stopped walking and looked at me uncertainly. I swallowed hard against the realization that I wanted to tell him. I wanted to let him in. Any question he asked at that moment I would answer honestly, thorns and all. He said, "You really like to spoil your dog, don't you?"

4

I pinched my lips to contain the gasp as I looked around and didn't know where we were. I had never walked this far before. We had only turned once – I was pretty sure of that anyway – so it wouldn't be hard to retrace our steps to the dog park. I limited myself to casual honesty about the situation. "Yeah, um... Paws has a lot of energy, but it's fine if we turn around now."

With three leashes that was easier said than done. We had to convince all the dogs that the new direction was better, and Baby wasn't falling for it. Once I got the other two moving, she plopped her butt on the sidewalk and refused to budge. Tracker only spent a few seconds coaxing her before he picked her up and positioned her in the crook of his right arm while he still held the leash in his left.

I noticed a couple about to pass us on the other side of the street. They were holding hands. I began to panic that Tracker would think I was wishing I wasn't holding leashes because I was getting ideas about him holding my hand and he wasn't thinking anything like that and didn't have any intention to ever be thinking anything like that and he was probably freaking out about me getting ideas like that when he only wanted to be friendly and hadn't planned on walking halfway around the city with his lazy, or maybe just old, dog. I needed to say something. "My last name is Fenley," I blurted.

"I noticed you didn't tell me before." He looked like a kid who just learned of a snow day. "What made you decide to tell me? Was it the band thing? You always wanted to know a guy who could play the drums, right?"

"I only decided you might not be an ax murderer."

"It's a start," he said, still grinning. "By the time we get back to the park, you'll be thinking I'm *definitely* not an ax murderer."

"Sure of yourself, huh? How do you plan to convince me?"

"Hmm…" He used the hand with a bunched up leash handle to readjust his hat, setting the bill a bit higher and knocking himself in the face with the leash in the process. "I guess I'm going to keep revealing fascinating things about myself until you either trust me or think I'm too boring to be anything scary."

"I'm looking forward to the next fascinating thing." I think I managed to include some sarcasm even though I was feeling totally not sarcastic.

"Okay… I, um… I think I know how to knit."

I'm not sure it counted as fascinating, but I liked the way he said it as though he really hoped I'd find it interesting. "You *think* you know how to knit?"

"Well, it's been a long time. I may have forgotten."

"So when did you learn how to knit?"

"A couple of my sisters were into knitting for a while and they showed me how. I was about… twelve and yarn made for cheap Christmas presents. I made a lot of scarves that year."

Will you show me sometime? That was the first thought that came into my head. I'd like to see him try to remember, but I couldn't say anything like that. I couldn't say anything that implied I expected to see him again. I waited too long to say anything at all because he kept talking.

"My birthday is New Year's Eve. That's sort of… I guess easy to remember isn't necessarily interesting. I… I like raisin cookies better than chocolate chip and I've been told that's unusual. Actually, I've been told that makes me weird, but I prefer to say it's unusual and not just weird. We had a cat when I was little and he ran in front of me and I tripped over him and thought I broke my arm. It was just a sprain, but I still had to wear a sling for a while. I've never actually broken a bone. Have you?"

"No."

"Because you've been careful or lucky?"

"Probably a little of both."

"Okay." Tracker drew in a long breath. It might have been

the first one he'd taken in a full minute. "Let me ask you something random," he said. "If you were at a restaurant and ordered, let's say… a burrito with chicken and they made a mistake and brought you beef. Assuming you have no dietary or religious reasons for not eating beef, you just felt like chicken that day, do you send it back to get what you wanted or eat the mistake?"

That question is weirder than liking raisin cookies. "That is random."

He nodded as though I had just complimented him.

"I would eat it," I said, "because I hate to see food going to waste. But if you want total honesty, I would likely spend the rest of the day thinking about that chicken I didn't get."

"I see. So you might be the sort of person who'd be too nice to tell a guy if he was bothering you. But let me ask you this… how did you choose your dog?"

"Paws?" My eyes traveled down the gray leash in my left hand to my dog, who was trotting along happily with her tongue hanging out. I'd have brought water for her if I had known we'd be walking so long.

"Yeah," he said. "Did you have a specific type of dog in mind or anything?"

"I wanted to get a bigger dog actually. I was nervous about living by myself and… well, I wasn't looking for a real guard dog. I just thought one with a nice, deep bark would make scary people reconsider breaking into my apartment. But I went to a shelter and Paws was one of the first dogs I met. We clicked. She just looked at me like she was ready to be mine, and I took her home as soon as I could."

"I'm sure she was grateful." Tracker shifted Baby to his other arm. "Do you want me to hold one of those leashes? I could take Sampson for a bit."

"Uh… okay." It did sound nice to have a break. Sampson's leash was looped around my wrist, and I let it slide to my fingers so I could pass it to Tracker. My brain didn't understand that incidental contact meant nothing. It lit up an obscene number of nerve endings when he took the leash from me.

We managed the transaction without stopping, and Tracker managed it without even slowing his stream of questions. "Do you cover your eyes if something scary is about to happen in a movie?"

"Not necessarily scary, but gory yes. I hide if I think there will be blood."

"Okay. What would you say is the nicest thing anyone has ever done for you?"

"I don't know." I shrugged and pointed at Sampson. "Hold his leash?"

Tracker stopped walking. I got a few steps ahead of him before I noticed and turned back. He was giving me a very strange look. "I can't tell if you're kidding," he said. "Tell me you're kidding because if that is seriously the nicest thing you can think of then I need to have a talk with the people in your life."

I started laughing. Only partly because he looked ready to beat some nice into people and that was an amusing thought. Mostly I laughed to cover how scared I was. That was the moment I knew I couldn't fool myself any longer. I *liked* this guy. I liked him more than I liked anyone in a long time, and I didn't want to admit that meant he could hurt me. "Yes, I'm kidding," I said. "That's just… that's a hard question to answer in the spur of the moment."

"All right." He put Baby back on the sidewalk before he began moving and she was willing to walk, though we went slower when she wasn't being carried. We walked in silence for at least half a block. I was sure he was making a deliberate effort not to bother me and his not talking was the only thing that was bothering me.

"Do you, um…" I wanted to try to ask him something random, but my mind was throwing out unrandom questions, all of them related to future possibilities that I wanted him to suggest first. I bent to pet Paws and clear my head. "How you doing, girl? We're getting close to home now." She seemed happy and I relaxed somewhat.

"Were you going to ask me something?" Tracker's blue eyes were hopeful under his hat.

My mind unlocked the door to random. "Have you ever gone back and finished one of those books from high school?"

"What do you mean?"

"You know, the books you were assigned to read in high school but you hadn't finished before the test so you quit reading them. Did you ever go back and finish one?"

He appeared scandalized and it was clearly an act. "What makes you think I didn't finish all of them in high school?"

"It's no fun to read a book someone else picked out for you," I said. "No one finishes all of them."

"No one?"

"All right. I'll ask you something else."

"No." He looked a little worried. "I'll be honest. I—"

"Too late." I held up the hand that was free now that I had only one dog under my control. "You missed that question. Try this… If someone were to make pancakes and waffles using the exact same batter, which would taste better?"

"The pancakes."

"You don't even want to think about that?"

"No way," he said. "You can't spread anything on waffles."

"I'm sorry. That is the wrong answer."

"What!?" He knew I was kidding that time.

"You don't spread syrup and that's the only thing that goes on either. Waffles hold the syrup better."

"Oh, this could be bad." Tracker shook his head sadly. "I thought we were getting along okay, but I'm not sure I can associate with a waffle person. Let me ask you something even more important."

We walked quietly while I waited with doubts about the importance of the next question. "Are you going to ask me?" I said eventually.

"I don't know. I'm a little worried about your answer."

"*I* think you're having trouble coming up with a question."

"Me? Never." That quick grin came out again and left a small shudder in my fingers. "Here goes… When you have a bowl of cereal, do you add the milk first or the cereal first?"

Something told me it would be fun to disagree with him, but I didn't know what answer he was looking for so I simply gave him the truth. "I pour the cereal first."

"Whew." He sort of slumped over with the phony effort of the sigh. "Maybe there's hope that you are a rational person after all."

~ 30 ~

I wasn't. We were passing the church and in sight of the dog park and he'd stopped walking. My imagination was dreaming up a wild scene where he said he just couldn't bear to finish the walk because he was enjoying my company too much for it to end. A rational person would ask why he stopped.

"I, uh…" He gestured to a black car parked on the street. "Well… that's my car, and I think Baby will hate me if I don't take her home now."

I looked at the little dog. She had flopped onto her side as soon as we stopped moving. I would have to let them go. "Thanks for holding Sampson," I said as I reclaimed the leash.

"You're welcome. I, um…" He bent as though he was going to pick up the dog but then stood up without her. "Okay, I think I was obvious as soon as I came out here to walk with you so I'm gonna go ahead and ask if we can exchange numbers to maybe talk again sometime without waiting to bump into each other."

He wanted my phone number. And something was obvious! Somewhere in my non-rational brain was a picture of the happy dance I was going to be doing when I was safely alone in my apartment. Paws didn't count as a witness. The rational side of me was trying to work out a few problems. My hands were full and there was no way I could talk at that moment without my voice coming out in an excited squeak. I inhaled slowly, calmly myself.

"Okay," I said. The word sounded mostly normal. "My hands are sort of tied up, but I can tell you my number and then I'll get yours when you call me." Should I have said if? Surely it wasn't presumptuous to expect a call after he asked for the number?

Tracker seemed to be trying to suppress a grin as he took out his phone and entered my number. I recognized the battle because my mouth was fighting a similar one. "Thanks," he said. Then he did lift Baby from the sidewalk. "I'll let you go and um, bye, Alexa."

He opened his car to put Baby in the backseat, and I began walking, working desperately to keep myself from looking back. His car drove past us shortly before we reached the crosswalk. I think I finally exhaled as it turned a corner.

5

*T*racker did not immediately call me or send me his number. I gradually went through what might have been every possible emotion about the number exchange being one-sided. I was happy about it at first because it was easier to have the proverbial ball so squarely in his court. And then I was nervous about him calling when I was somehow unprepared for a conversation. And of course I meant more nervous and unprepared than I would be no matter when he called.

It was about the time I was getting ready for bed on Friday that I mentally screamed at myself for not getting his number in person. I feared I had given him mine incorrectly. Then I felt relief that I didn't have his number because calling to make sure he had the right one for me would have been a tad embarrassing.

That's not true.

It would have gone right past embarrassing to downright pathetic. I woke up with a little more peace and some hope that I might just run into him with Baby again and have nothing to worry about. And then I started to think maybe I didn't want him to call me at all when we probably had different goals for the relationship anyway. And at some point I sat on my sofa holding my phone and staring at it and trying to convince myself how dumb it was to be depressed over a guy I still barely knew.

In my haste to prove to myself I could think about something other than the endearing guy with the name I couldn't say without thinking he should be wearing a collar, I let my mind replay the last conversation I'd had with my mom. She asked me for the fourth time during that call why Megan might be avoiding her.

"I don't know, Mom," I had said. "She's not talking to me either." *And you know that.*

"How long do you think this is gonna go on?"

"I don't know." *Stop asking me that.* That's when I started to get irritated.

"She could stay with me if she's having money problems again."

"I think she knows that."

"Then why won't she ask?"

Why won't you ask me why I'm raising my voice? Do you even notice this is upsetting me? "Maybe she doesn't want your help."

"What if she needs it though?" Maybe Mom didn't notice because she was more worked up than I was. Her voice edged near hysterical. "What if she's staying with another guy who doesn't treat her right?"

I don't want to talk about Megan. I don't want to talk about Megan. "Mom, I don't want to talk about Megan anymore."

"She's your sister! Don't you care what happens to her?"

"Yes, I care." It didn't sound like I cared. "But I can't do anything about it. It's not my fault Megan is who she is."

"Then it's my fault? You blame me for raising a daughter who—?"

"I didn't say that, Mom. I—"

"I did the best I could, you know. Maybe if your father had been around. But you can't make a man stay if he wants to leave."

I can't talk to you. "I'm not going to call you next Sunday." I hadn't meant to say it in anger. It was supposed to sound like a reasoned decision and it came out like I wanted to punish her. She reacted before I could explain.

"You're going to cut me off, too? Just like that!?"

"It's not... I... I'm tired of having the same argument every week. I want to take a week off to see if we can think of something different to talk about." *Maybe you'll even ask how I'm doing for a change.*

Then I hung up on her. I hung up on my own mother. She had every right to be angry with me. It had been three days since I left her a message and I'd gotten no response. I sat there trying to decide if I wanted to call her again.

The truth was uncomfortable. I wanted to talk to my mom but even more than that, I wanted to hold on to the feeling that

if we didn't talk, it was on her. I had already apologized. I put
away my phone to focus on the simplest relationship I had.

"Hey, girl," I said to Paws.

She picked her head up off my lap.

"Let's go to the park again."

She jumped up and ran to the door. I didn't know if she
understood the word go or the word park. They likely meant the
same thing to her anyway. I clipped on her leash and we went
across the street. It was full of dogs and people. "Lots of
friends for you today," I said.

Paws ran in a sort of zigzag line for a few moments, and I
wasn't sure if that was her being excited or her practicing
avoiding those friends. I tried to get us through the gate quickly
in case someone had a dog like Sampson who might try to
escape.

There were a few faces I knew as regulars, including the Jack
woman. I sighed and averted my eyes because I couldn't look at
her without thinking Jack! I didn't know her name, but I knew
her dog's name was Jack! and everyone at the park knew her
dog's name was Jack! because the poor little terrier couldn't do
anything without her yelling Jack!

She yelled for him if he picked up a stick. She yelled for him
if he was running too fast. She yelled for him if he jumped on
another dog, even if the other dog wanted to play. And it never
did any good. Jack would go right on doing whatever he was
doing – which most people would call being a dog – regardless
of how many times she screamed his name.

I ignored her and all the other people to play with my own
dog. She brought me a stick as soon as I let her off leash. "I'm
not going to chase you," I told her.

She wagged her tail a little faster.

"You're spoiled now, aren't you? Tracker chased you one
time and now you think you can get me to try to get your stick."

Paws took a step closer and turned her head, almost as
though she was giving me the stick. She was too cute. And we
both knew it wasn't Tracker who had spoiled her. I made a grab
for the stick and she lunged away and ran a circle around me. I
ran after her. It was more of a jog because I knew I couldn't

catch her and thought it best not to risk tripping over one of the other dogs. Paws was satisfied to have me in the game.

When I grew tired of chasing her, I tried to fool her with a different stick. Either I was not as good an actor or she'd figured out the trick. She wouldn't drop hers. I sat on a bench, and she ran off to get someone with four legs to chase her.

My phone rang and it was an unknown number. My instinct was to let it go to voicemail because Paws had helped me forget for a moment that I was waiting for a call from an unknown number.

My free hand began to tap nervously on the bench as I answered.

"Alexa?"

"Yes. This is Alexa."

"Hi, it's Tracker."

"Hi, uh…" I just couldn't make myself say it. "Hi."

"Is this a bad time?"

"No. I'm just watching Paws run around."

"You're at the park, huh?"

"Yeah. Second time today as a matter of fact."

"Good weather for it."

The silence stretched on long enough for me to feel like it was my turn to say something. But I couldn't just agree that summer was nice after needing a minute to think about that.

Tracker said, "What is that dog doing?"

"What dog?"

"I'm assuming that woman is yelling at her dog. What's he doing?"

I had tuned her out, but apparently the Jack woman could be annoying even through the phone. I moved my eyes from Paws to the little terrier so I could explain. "Well," I said, "as far as I can tell, the woman is simply trying to alert the park to the fact that her dog is sniffing another dog's butt."

His laugh came through the phone and softened something inside me. "Sounds exciting. No wonder you like it there so much."

"Yep. You and Baby are missing out." Did that sound like an invitation? It wasn't my intent but I would be thrilled if he took it that way.

He didn't. Though after a pause he said, "I suppose this is too short notice to ask if you're free for dinner tonight."

"I'm afraid it is." I was as disappointed as I sounded. I was serving dinner at a homeless shelter that night. I was only on the schedule one Saturday a month and it felt like horrible luck to be that one.

"Okay," he said. "Uh… you do the coffee and donuts thing at church, right?"

"I do."

"Will you be there tomorrow?"

"I plan to." Hope was coming back. He wasn't taking my not tonight to mean never.

"Maybe… um, maybe I can find you there and we can make a plan to do something later in the day or something."

"I think that's a good idea."

"Good, I'll… I'll see you then."

I put my phone away and found that I had a lot more energy to run around with Paws. We stayed almost until dinnertime. I got sunburn on my shoulders and I didn't care.

That's not true.

I cared a little about the sunburn when my shirt started rubbing on it. But I was serving meals to people who might not know where their next one would come from and that definitely put things into perspective.

I snuggled up with my dog in front of the TV after my volunteer duty. I wondered if I should have suggested to Tracker that we do something after dinner. I wasn't much of a night owl though and he should know that. He should know right away anything that he might consider a deal-breaker because I didn't want to get my hopes up any higher before a fall.

I forced myself not to think about him and since I didn't want to think about my mom, I ended up calling my dad. I told him that Paws was almost due for her heartworm medicine and he told me what he had for dinner. I asked if he'd finished a library book he'd mentioned a few weeks ago and he didn't ask me anything. Most of the time, my dad was the easiest person to talk to.

6

I wore my favorite dress to church on Sunday. It was midnight blue and fitted on top with a flowy skirt. Though I only ever wore it to church, it made me picture a romantic and dimly lit meal. I stood in front of my mirror and felt pretty until I started to blush because I was picturing that romantic meal with a certain person that I hoped to see soon.

I put Paws in her crate and said, "You'll be thinking about me while I'm gone, right? Hoping things are going well?"

She turned around and settled into a ball on her blanket. I latched the crate and left.

I sat in the same general area of the church I usually sat. I faced the altar and struggled against the urge to feel weird about that. I always came in early and sat still, trying to prepare myself for mass. I was not in the habit of looking around or caring much about who was sitting nearby so it should not have been weird to not do that. I didn't know if Tracker was going to church before or after coffee. I didn't know if he was somewhere in the hundreds of people filing into the church. But he might be. He might be looking at me, wondering if I wondered if he was there.

Our Father, who art in heaven... I closed my eyes and continued. There was nothing like rote prayer to focus a person on why she was in church. And even if I was only distracted and not focused, at least it was a holy distraction.

I didn't see Tracker as I made my way over to the parish hall. I didn't see him inside either. I got some coffee and sat at my usual table. "Hi, Suzy," I said as I sat. "How was your week?"

"Pretty good. How about you?"

"It was fine." I chanced a look right into her eyes, testing her theory that she'd be able to tell if I had met someone.

She only nodded. "We'll be quiet this week since Maria and Antonio won't be joining us."

"That's right," I said. "They said they were going Saturday this week."

"Hello, ladies." Joyce's cane hit the side of the table as she set it down. A young man was pulling out her chair for her. She moaned as she settled into it. "Austin, honey," she said, "I want you to meet some of my friends. That's Suzy and this here is Alexa."

Austin? She called him Austin. Was this *the* Austin, the wonderful grandson she'd been talking up for the last two years? This was the day she picked to finally introduce him?

"Hi," he said. "It's nice to meet both of you. I'm sorry I can't stay."

He couldn't stay. I smiled at him. "Glad to finally put a face with the name. Your grandmother is a fan."

"I'm sure she is." He sighed as he said it, probably knowing she was trying to play match-maker. "Hope you enjoy your coffee, Gran."

Austin waved as he left us, and I watched him out the door because he was eating a donut. Maybe if there were only going to be three of us – no sign of Linda yet – I could finally get a donut.

Suzy's nails were tapping the side of her cup and they were purple today. "So that was Austin," she said, looking at me as though I should have found the two-second conversation enlightening.

"My oldest grandchild," Joyce said. The pride in her voice tipped immediately into irritation. "Now if he would just hurry up and get married," she shot a sharp glance at me, "I could start hoping for babies."

It sounded to me as though she was already hoping. I felt kind of sorry for Austin. She had said he was twenty-four. My opinion was that was old enough to get married but not nearly old enough for anyone to be freaking out about his not being married. I mean, that was a year younger than me and I wasn't freaking out. About not being married anyway.

I was kind of obsessing about the way Joyce kept setting her paper cup on the table so that it covered a chip in the surface. I didn't know if it was odd for her to keep doing that or odd for me to be grateful about her doing that. Maybe we were both odd and that was why we were friends even though she was old enough to be my grandmother. I stopped freaking out about the chip in the table and turned to pay attention to what Joyce and Suzy were talking about. I turned to Suzy as she said, "Wait. There he goes."

I looked between her and Joyce.

Suzy noticed my confusion. "Don't look," she whispered. "But there's a guy walking past us and I think he's holding a ring that a girl just gave to him. As in, gave *back* to him."

"Oh, dear," Joyce muttered, likely feeling bad for the poor guy's grandmother. She kept her eyes on her carefully positioned cup.

I watched Suzy. Her eyes traveled momentarily back to where the girl must have been. I didn't want to look. I tried not to look. Eventually my eyes seemed to move on their own in that direction. Instead of taking in what Suzy had mentioned, I saw past the other table to where a guy was standing by himself and looking at me.

It was Tracker. It took me a moment to recognize him without the baseball hat. His hair was dark and very short. It was fluffy, like it would have been curly if it was longer. He cleaned up nicely for church. There was something almost shy in his eyes that said he really wanted me to come over there. It was surprising after all the times he'd approached me at the park.

But it was perfect. He was standing right next to the donut table.

"If you two will excuse me," I said, "I think I feel like having a donut today. Can I get either of you anything while I'm up?"

Suzy shook her head at me and Joyce said, "No, thank you, dear."

I took my cup with me and concentrated on not spilling it on myself more than I had any other Sunday and it was only half full.

I was about to say hello when Tracker said, "Wow, you look nice." And then he looked like he wanted to take it back. I wasn't sure if he hadn't meant to say that out loud or if he only hadn't meant to sound so surprised. I guess he was used to seeing me at a dog park, too.

"Thanks," I said quickly so we could move on. "Were you at the 8:30 or are you going to the 10:30?"

"8:30."

I looked at the donuts and knew I was out of luck. The only ones left were covered in powdered sugar. There was no way I could eat one of those standing up without turning the front of my dark blue dress into a blue and white speckled dress. "Me, too," I said to continue the conversation as though I wasn't thinking about donuts and my lack of one.

I put my attention on Tracker, which might have been a mistake. His shirt was light green, untucked, and had short sleeves. All those details were fine with me, but the buttons down the front got me. Each one had four holes and was stitched on with an X. Except for the top one. The highest buttoned one anyway. It was sideways like a plus sign. I was going to be looking at that all day. Or I might be if I could get out of my head and convince Tracker he wanted to spend even part of the day with me. "So you, uh… do you usually go to the 8:30?"

"No," he said. "But I thought you did."

"Did I tell you that?" I didn't remember telling him that.

He smiled sort of guiltily. "I may have seen you before."

I was confused about how he had seen me if he wasn't there. I felt my phone vibrating in the bag under my arm though. "Excuse me a sec," I said as I pulled it out to check. I didn't recognize the number so I stuffed it back in my bag.

"I'm guessing you want to give your dog a little exercise before you do anything else," Tracker said, reminding me that we might be about to have a date and making me forget what we'd just been talking about. "Maybe we could stop at the park and then go somewhere for lunch. Do you want to change first?"

If we were going out, there was no way he was going to be more dressed up than I was. "No," I said. "It's dry today. I can take Paws in my church clothes."

"So I could wait for you at the park while you get her and

then, um…" He looked uncertain. He was also looking behind me.

I turned to see Monsignor Loy approaching. "Good morning, my sheep." He called everyone my sheep because he was terrible with names. It wasn't condescending at all; it sounded as though he really wanted to care for his flock. And as far as I knew no one minded about the names because he remembered *everything* else. He asked after job searches and health problems and family visits. I'd even heard him wish Maria and Antonio a happy anniversary.

"Good morning," I said.

Tracker nodded a similar greeting.

Monsignor Loy picked up a donut and focused on Tracker. "Would you permit me a private word with the accidental Catholic here?" He waved his hand at me.

"Of course." Tracker turned to me. "Meet you outside when you're done?"

I nodded at him and turned to the priest feeling a little anxious. If he was still concerned about me I must have inadvertently exaggerated my family issues. Surely he had parishioners dealing with more serious problems. "How are you?" he asked me pointedly.

"I'm better. Really."

"All that anger just up and disappeared, huh?" He smiled and he clearly saw right through me.

I shook my head. "I am trying to talk to her."

"With God's help you'll get there."

"I did hear from my sister." A sharp voice in the back of my head urged me to be fully honest with the man wearing a white collar. "I mean, it was three words but it was something and I don't expect us to have a healthy relationship overnight. It's a step. And I'm still praying."

"As am I," he said. "I believe you can talk to the young man waiting for you if you need to."

"Maybe," I said.

"And have a donut." Monsignor Loy took a large bite and still managed to talk around it without spraying me with sugar. "Helps with almost everything," he said. He did look peaceful as he tasted it. As he walked away, I was tempted to risk the mess on my dress for a bite. But I couldn't throw away a half-eaten donut and Tracker was waiting for me and he was going to be waiting for me to get Paws and take her back home and my phone was trying to tell me that unknown number had left a message.

"Fine," I said to no one before I moved away from the sugar-covered temptations. I pulled out my phone. I told Suzy and Joyce that I would see them next week before I stepped outside with my phone pressed to my ear. I expected a wrong number to be the most interesting message, but it was for me.

A female voice said, "Alexa? This is Sheila... uh... Fenley. I'm calling to let you know that your dad... our dad has had a heart attack. We're at the hospital waiting for some tests but he's stable. He doesn't seem to be in immediate danger. Your mom thought you'd want to know but... well, she gave me your number." Sheila told me which hospital and the room number before she hung up.

I moved the phone in front of me so I could see it. The voicemail lady was listing options that didn't make a lot of sense. The half-sister I'd never met had just calmly informed me that our dad was in the hospital. She was the one to tell me because my mom was still not speaking to me even in an emergency. My life was a big, hot, steaming pile of screwed up.

Tracker was suddenly kneeling on the sidewalk in front of me. When had I sat down? My eyes involuntarily took in that button with the crooked X of thread before they moved to his face.

Whoa! He looked terrified. His mouth was moving, but all I could hear was the faint sound of the voicemail lady still politely telling me I could save that message. It seemed to be coming at me through a rush of wind.

"Alexa?" There was Tracker's voice. "Alexa? What's wrong?"

"My dad had a heart attack."

"Is he... how bad is it?"

I felt my head shaking. "They're doing tests."

"Okay. So you're going to the hospital? Can I drive you?" He put his hand out to help me up. I didn't feel romantic flutters when I took it – only strength – and I kept a tight grip even once I was standing.

He pulled me towards the parking lot. "Come on," he said. "I'm going to drive you."

He thought I meant the hospital in Thompsonville. "It's two hours away."

"It doesn't matter." Tracker took me to the same car I'd seen when he was with Baby. He opened the front door for me. I was able to tell him the name of the hospital and he put the address into his GPS and started driving without another word.

The fog or the panic or whatever had been wrong with my brain began to clear before we left the city. I remembered my responsibilities. "What about Paws?" I said.

"You took her out right before church, right? And fed her?"

"Yeah. I did."

"And she's usually alone while you're at work, right?"

"Yeah."

"This probably won't be any longer than that so she'll be okay. And we have time to figure something out if it looks like it'll take longer."

I nodded. I hoped he was right. He said it very practically, as though he'd already considered my dog while I was staring out the window. Maybe it wasn't right for me to accept so much kindness. "What about you?" I asked.

His eyes darted to me with a question then back to the road.

"I mean you shouldn't be going so far out of your way for me. I'm feeling better so you can take me back to get my car."

"No." The word was definitive by itself, but he began to elaborate. "I'm not leaving you alone right now. What if, God forbid, you get more bad news when we get there? Besides, we're already fifteen minutes into the drive. If I turn around, that's another half hour that Paws will have to wait for you."

I had to admit he had good arguments. And that as long as he was driving I was stuck. I still wanted to make sure we covered everything. "What about Baby?"

"Oh." He winced and looked very uncomfortable. Had he thought about my dog before he thought about his own? "Alexa," he said slowly, very slowly, "I... please don't be upset but I kind of... misled you about something and I guess this is as good a time as any to confess."

"Okay?" I prompted.

He took a deep breath and began talking faster. "Baby's not my dog. She belongs to my sister. She – my sister – just had a baby. A baby baby. I was watching the dog to, you know, help out a little and I'm sorry I didn't tell you that right away. But Baby is with my sister now so she'll be taken care of today."

7

I wasn't thrilled about having been misled. I suppose I never asked him straight out if Baby belonged to him, and it was a nice thing for him to do for his sister. In fact, I thought it was strange that he hadn't mentioned that nice thing when he was trying to convince me he was harmless.

"You're not mad, are you?" Tracker asked. He sounded worried. He looked miserable at the thought and that made it difficult to be angry. Mostly though, I just had too much on my mind already to leave room for anger towards the guy who had done so much more right than he had wrong.

I let him off the hook. "No," I said.

"Are you sure?"

My no hadn't come out very convincingly. "Yes. I mean, I'm sure I'm not mad about the dog. I'm just really upset with myself at the moment."

"Why are you upset with yourself?"

"Because we're on our way to the hospital, and I'm more worried about the family drama that might be waiting for me than I am about my dad's health." I sighed and felt lousy for saying that out loud. "Don't get me wrong. I do hope my dad will be okay. I'm praying for him. But I don't know who all will be there, and I'm afraid there might be some kind of ugly scene and... *I hate arguing.*"

"Do you want to tell me about it?"

I did. But there was so much to tell. If I started talking I might not stop before we got there. And it was a long drive.

"Is that a no?" Tracker asked gently. "You don't have to tell me."

"I want to but I don't know where to start."

He shrugged. "Anywhere you want."

"All right." Since we were going to see my dad, he seemed like a logical beginning. I tried to blow out the fear that Tracker would no longer be on my side after I opened up to him and dove into the first installment of my life's story. "My dad has been married three times. First he was married to a woman named Joan. They had two kids, a girl and a boy. Then he married my mom and had me and my sister. He left us when I was nine. Megan was almost eleven. When I was sixteen, he got married again, but that marriage only lasted two years and they had no kids.

"So I've always had this extra brother and sister that I knew *of* but I didn't know and that's been... well, awkward at the best of times. My dad had pictures of them. I knew how old they were. They're seven and ten years older than me. And I remember being confused about why he went to visit them without us until... Well, until I got to experience a dad who only visited. I remember asking my mom, pestering her about why I couldn't meet them, before I was old enough to understand that it might be weird for her to talk about my siblings who were not her kids.

"Eventually, she told me that I couldn't meet them because they didn't to meet me. No one has ever explicitly told me why but I know my parents got married immediately after my dad's first divorce was final and that Megan was born only five months later. So I suspect that my mom either was the cause or was believed to be the cause of that marriage breaking up and his first kids didn't want anything to do with her and with us by extension."

"That's not right," Tracker said. "Even if your mom had been involved with your dad when he was still married, you didn't have anything to do with it."

"I know, but I understand why they'd be mad at me anyway. I blamed my sister when my dad left. Sort of. Megan and I have never gotten along. I think I blamed her and she blamed me – not because either of us really believed that – but because it gave us one more thing to fight about. It's easier to be angry than to be hurt."

"Wow." He gave me a glance that said he was impressed. "That's a wise thing for you to say."

I shrugged. I didn't feel wise. I felt like someone who knew that hurting was difficult.

"So you think your dad's other kids will be at the hospital?"

"Yeah. Sheila – that's my half-sister's name – she's the one who called me. I think that affected me more than the news itself. I figured I'd probably meet her only at our dad's funeral." Why did I say that? I don't want to think about a funeral right now. "Or maybe I'd never meet her."

"People tend to be tense at a hospital. I understand you being worried about it not being the ideal setting for an introduction."

"My even bigger concern is my mom."

"Will she…? I guess I don't know what kind of terms she and your dad are on now."

"Surprisingly good, all things considered." I paused a moment to think about how to describe it. "They've never been screaming match kind of people, more like quiet resentment kind of people. They've always done their best to be civil in public, and I think as the years have gone by it's become less and less of an act. There will likely be more tension between her and me."

"Oh." Tracker appeared to hesitate while he formed a question. "Has your relationship with her always been a struggle or is there something recent that set things off?"

"A little of both. Mom was always… preoccupied with Megan. My sister had a very rough start in school. Because she was only a year ahead of me, we ended up in the same class right away and I lorded it over her something awful. I bragged to everyone about how I was smarter than my big sister and I wish someone would have told me to shut up. I don't know if it would have done any good because I was just a kid, but I never… It *never* occurred to me how it might make her feel.

"A teacher finally figured out when we were in I think fifth grade that she was dyslexic. They tried to help her, but by then she was already… well, not interested in doing better in school. She wanted to be the class clown and had lots of, uh, behavior problems. I was always jealous of the extra attention Megan got for acting out and I think she might have been jealous of me for being perceived as the good kid. If I'm sounding wise again it's because I've been talking to Monsignor Loy about this."

"Is that when you told him about the Bible study?"

"What do you mean?"

Tracker's mouth closed a little tighter like he was trying not to smile in the middle of a serious discussion. "He… he called you the accidental Catholic this morning."

"Oh, yeah." He hadn't been referring to the Bible study. "That's not… the Bible study was nondenominational. That was how I became a Christian, but I also… um, became more specifically Catholic sort of… well, also by accident."

Tracker laughed at me and apologized at the same time. "I'm sorry," he said. "It's just the way you said it like… I'm sorry, it's not funny. It just sounds like you think that's weird, but I don't think anyone really sets out to convert unless they're doing it for someone else and that's… well, different. Take a break from the family stuff to tell me how you accidentally became Catholic. Please."

"All right." I liked the way he said please. Actually, I liked the way he laughed at me, too. That was a bad sign. "When I was getting close to graduation and was planning to move to Thompsonville, my friend in the Bible study gave me lots of advice on finding a new church there. She told me to visit several before I made a decision and she… um, she included a specific warning *against* any Catholic churches. She said it was some sort of cult and not real Christians at all. But then I moved into that apartment complex and Sacred Heart was right next door. I couldn't resist checking it out. And I liked it. And I was confused. The giant crucifix is like the first thing you see, right? I thought, Jesus is front and center at this church, how is it not Christian? So I found an ad in the bulletin for RCIA classes starting up and I went because I thought I would find out why I needed to find a different church and then… well, it connected all the dots for me in a way I didn't expect and I officially joined the church a year ago last Easter."

"I'm glad you did," he said, then looked as though he might have said something wrong. "Not that… I don't have a… It's just nice that we have that in common."

"I agree." It was nice that we'd both consider marriage a sacrament because then he...

Marriage? My mouth went dry and my head started spinning. Who put that thought in my head? My husband was going to be one family member I got to choose and I intended to make that choice very, *very* carefully.

My mind drifted to my history in this field of choosing a new family member. I'd been on a few dates here and there but only had two significant relationships. The first guy I had been dating almost five months when he asked me if I'd thought any about us getting married.

I said no because he wasn't proposing. He asked the question out of the blue like he was asking me what I wanted on my pizza. I wasn't prepared to declare that I thought I might want to marry him if he was about to tell me that he hadn't even thought about it. He said it was better that he knew where he stood with me and left me without knowing where he stood. I tried to call him, but I think he blocked my number. Maybe he hadn't been thinking marriage and took the excuse to get out. Only hindsight gave me that comfort. And it wasn't much.

The next breakup was a different type of awful. We were together about eight months. He said he couldn't handle the pressure of being the only relationship in my life on steady ground. That's right. He knew he was the only person I was always happy to see and that made him want out. Maybe I should have been glad to see him go, but I wasn't. I cried a lot and I came very close to failing the class he was in with me because I was no longer happy when I saw him. I guess he got everything he wanted.

In a memory that still made me cringe, I asked him if we could try again now that we had a breakup to complicate our relationship. I didn't really want that but I was lonely and confused.

Now I was sitting in a car with a guy who seemed to be on a mission to make me like him, and it was working. All of my senses seemed to be pointing to his side of the car. I couldn't deny the physical pull. He felt like a real possibility. But a possibility for what? For ripping out that last piece of my heart that still clung to hope? I couldn't believe I let the M word into my head so soon. We were going to need to spend a lot more time not arguing before I let it happen again.

"So you were talking about your mom," Tracker said, "and it sounded like something changed more recently to make you nervous about seeing her today."

"My sister sort of... went off the grid. She was evicted from her apartment because she had gotten behind on her rent and she refused to give my mom or anyone else her new address. Then she stopped answering or returning calls. This was just before Christmas and my mom has been flipping out ever since. I got in the habit of calling to check in with her every Sunday afternoon and after Megan... It's the only thing she wants to talk about. I get that she's stressing out about what my sister might be doing. I worry, too. It just doesn't do any good to yell at each other every week about what could happen so I tried to suggest we make a change to break up the pattern and it didn't go well. Mom thought I was trying to say I didn't want to talk to her at all."

"That sounds hard. I'm sorry you're having to deal with all that." Tracker looked my way for the second he could take his eyes off the road and I saw compassion and not judgment.

"Thank you," I said. "I mean it. Thank you for listening to me and for driving me. This is nothing like how you planned to spend the day, is it?"

"Not exactly. I did... well, you know I was hoping to spend some time with you and we are doing that. I do wish you were happier about it."

"I am happy about, um... you're kinda the bright spot. Especially if you're going to tell me a funny story now." I tried to offer an ingratiating smile, which I think he caught out of the corner of his eye because he also smiled.

"Oh, yes," he said. "Nothing is easier than coming up with a funny story on cue."

"I'll give you minute."

"I'm sure that will help." His sarcasm lifted my spirits a touch already, as did how happy he looked when I called him the bright spot. "This isn't a story, but I think it's funny that my nephew, who is three, has been using the word whobody."

"Whobody?"

"Yeah, like whobody wants to read me this book?"

"That is funny."

"Oh, I thought of something." Tracker's face showed excitement and then uncertainty. "It might be one of those things where you had to be there but... Okay, so this one time my grandmother came over to babysit and she decided to make us some cookies as a treat. I don't know exactly how it happened, but I think it involved at least one unlabeled canister. She ended up making them with salt in place of the sugar. She tasted one and realized her mistake and she was just going to throw them out, but a couple of my sisters were curious and wanted to taste them. They both spit them out so I didn't try one.

"But then my other sister, Kayley, she came in and said everyone was making a big deal over nothing. They were peanut butter cookies, and she was like 'People like salt on peanuts so they can't be that bad.' So of course being the nice loving siblings that we are..." Tracker flashed that wink-in-a-grin at me. This was a good story. "We dared her to eat a whole cookie. You could see how disgusted she was from the very first taste, but she did it anyway. She forced herself to eat that whole cookie just to prove she was right about them being not that bad. Then I think she drank about a half a gallon of milk trying to get the taste out of her mouth."

"That's really terrible," I said.

"I'm glad I could make you laugh." Though I think he might have enjoyed the story even more than I did.

"Can you do it again?" *I love that you can make me laugh.*

"Let me think." He stared ahead while his mind worked. He told me several more stories from his childhood. Some were funny and others less so. All of them made me glad I wasn't making the drive by myself. When we got close to the hospital, Tracker went through a drive-through for lunch. I had just polished off the burger when he stopped in front of the main entrance.

"I'll drop you off here," he said, "and then find a place to park. I'll let you go in by yourself so you can have some privacy with your family and... Well, this way you don't have to explain the random guy tagging along."

"What are you going to do while I'm in there?"

"Don't worry. I can amuse myself. And you have my number, right?"

I nodded.

"Call me or text when you're ready to go or if you need anything. I'll stay close."

He'd stay close? That felt like a promise for more than just an afternoon. I wanted to trust it so much I had a vision of leaning over to his side of the car to kiss him with my thanks. I don't know if that would have been bold or just stupid, but it didn't matter since I only said the word and left the kiss in my head. I grabbed my bag and jumped out of the car.

8

I got directions from someone behind a large desk but apparently made at least one wrong turn. I found myself facing a closed door with warnings posted about setting off an alarm if I opened it. That seemed almost as bad as me thinking about kissing the guy who was only being nice. Maybe. There were indications that his interest lay beyond friendship. I was just too scared to believe it.

But I needed to stop thinking about my guy problem if I was ever going to solve my lost in a hospital problem. I tried to make my way back to the front desk. On the way, I was stopped by a nurse who must have recognized the bewildered look on my face. He escorted me part of the way to my dad's room and assured me I'd find it from there. He was right.

I stood outside a closed door with the number 412 next to it. I knocked so lightly even I couldn't hear the sound. A quick mental prayer/pep talk got me to knock with more confidence.

"Come in," I heard from inside. It was my dad's voice. Was he alone?

I walked in as though I didn't care one way or the other. Dad was sitting up in a bed on the far side of the room. An empty bed was between us. Tan dividing curtains hung pushed up against the wall in at least four places. A younger version of my dad was sitting in a chair near the window. He stood as I entered, and I didn't know who I should address first.

"Alexa!" Dad sounded surprised to see me. "You didn't need to drive all the way over here."

"How are you, Dad?" I walked closer to his bed, trying not to be as uncomfortable as Mike looked.

"Fine, honey. You really didn't need to come. They're going to let me out tomorrow."

We both know I had to come in case you weren't fine. "When your dad is in the hospital," I said, "you have to visit him. I think it might be a rule."

He smiled at me like he was posing for a picture. "Sit down then, since you're here."

I took a chair between the beds, and Mike reclaimed the one by the window. I needed to say something to him before the elephant took up any more space in the room. "Is he telling the truth, Mike? Is he fine?"

"I think so." Mike looked at my dad – our dad – then back at me. "I was here when the doctor talked to him. He said it was technically a heart attack but very minor. Dad is… um, he's supposed to be careful about his diet and such from now on."

"And you're going to follow those instructions, Dad?"

He reached out and patted my hand. "Of course, honey."

"Okay, um… and how are you doing?" I looked at the man my dad linked to me.

"Not bad," Mike said.

"And your wife?"

"She's good. Home with the kids right now."

"Yeah, Dad… uh…" I gestured to the guy in the bed. "He told me when they were born. How old are they now?"

"Bailey is three," Mike said, "and Baxter will have his first birthday in just a few weeks."

"I can't believe it's been a year already," Dad said.

I was thinking more that I couldn't believe it had been three.

"Would you—?" Mike cut himself off. He was looking at me and I tried to look as though he was welcome to finish the thought. "Would you have any interest in meeting my kids?"

"I would."

"Good, I… I'd been thinking about calling you again. Has your number changed?"

"No."

"So if I invited you over for dinner sometime maybe…" His eyebrows lifted to add the question mark.

"Yeah," I said. "I'd like that."

"Good. I was actually just getting ready to leave, and I didn't want you to think I left because you got here." Mike stood up again as he finished talking.

We had an awkward goodbye. I really didn't know if the thought of getting together with him later improved the tension or not. Then it was just me and my dad.

We chatted a good twenty minutes about nothing. He told me about the stream of visitors he'd had. My mom had only stayed a few minutes. Sheila left right before I got there. One of his golfing buddies had even come to see him. I did not ask him to tell me the story of how he ended up in that sterilized bed. I think he appreciated that as much as I did him not asking me why Megan hadn't been in. He kept saying I didn't need to entertain him and I took that to mean he'd be just as happy watching TV. I pushed my chair back against the wall and prepared to say goodbye.

"That God thing is still working for you I guess?"

"Yeah." I put my bag over my shoulder without even looking at him.

"You gonna add me to the list of demands?"

I don't know why I didn't just say okay, but I tried not to sound argumentative when I said, "That's not how it works, Dad."

He didn't respond with words and kept looking at me with something like curiosity.

Can I really explain it? "I PUSH," I said tentatively.

"Push?"

"I don't remember where I first heard the acronym. It means Pray Until Something Happens. The something is what's important. It's not always… like I might be praying about a stressful situation at work and maybe it gets resolved and maybe I simply figure out a way to not let it bother me anymore." *Or maybe I'm praying about being lonely and right when I think I've found some peace with what might never happen, a guy with a dog's name shows up to confuse me.*

"Listing demands would do as much good," Dad said, a clear edge to his voice. It was time to change the subject.

"So will you need a ride if you get to go home tomorrow?"

"Mike will be back to pick me up."

"Good. And you don't need anything else right now?"

"Go on," he said. "I know you have a long drive."

I just waved from where I was. He might have had another heart attack if I'd tried to do something radical like give him a hug. I wandered the hall until I found an exit. It wasn't the door I came in, but it didn't have an alarm on it. The hospital had been cold so at first I was glad to be outside. Then the afternoon sun began to plaster my dress to my back. I took out my phone as I walked and texted Tracker: `I'm ready to go when you are. Where are you?`

I had almost reached the front entrance when I got his reply: `I'm in the lobby. Where are you?`

I sent only: `coming`. He may have been reading that one word when I walked in and found him at the end of a row of chairs.

He got to his feet quickly and squinted at me. "Why are you coming from outside?"

"These hallways are confusing. I thought I could find my way faster if I just walked around the building."

"Okay." Tracker bit his lip nervously. "So… how did it go?"

"Oh. Dad's fine. As fine as someone in the hospital can be I guess. They said it was minor, whatever that means, and if nothing changes he'll be released tomorrow."

"Good. That's good. You want to head back?" He nodded to the door and kept talking as we left together. "And how was… everything else?"

I felt like folding in on myself. "Would you believe I got all worked up for nothing?"

"Well, that's not… I mean you didn't *want* an ugly scene, right?"

"No."

"What happened? Did you see your mom at all?"

I shook my head. "My… Mike, who is from my dad's first marriage, he was the only one there and he was on his way out when I arrived."

"I think he's the only one you didn't talk about on the way here. Had you met him before?"

"A few times. He reached out to me first near the end of my freshman year of college. He said he'd always been curious about me, and if I felt the same maybe we could get together."

Tracker nodded that he was listening, and it looked as though he actually wanted to know.

"We met for dinner and it was uncomfortable but not... we got along okay. It was just all tense and overly polite. I think everyone at the restaurant thought we were on a really bad date and that made it more awkward, but we tried to laugh about that. I saw him again about a year later when he invited me to his wedding. There were so many people I didn't get to talk to him much. I appreciated being included though. I saw Sheila there. She walked away when I tried to approach her. The last time I saw Mike was right before I moved to Thompsonville. I had dinner with him and his wife. She was expecting their first kid and having a third person seemed to take the pressure off."

"I can see that." Tracker fumbled keys out of his pocket. He unlocked his car and opened the door for me. It felt... Well, he might have been the only person to ever open a car door for me and I wasn't sure what to do with my hands.

The drive home seemed much shorter. We didn't talk about my family anymore, and we didn't spend much time on his family either. He told me about some of the people who worked with him and I told him about the cycling class and about how I had tried and failed at kickboxing before that. We talked about an odd-shaped building and an obnoxious billboard and speculated on what might be growing in a field we passed.

A sense of disappointment I'd been fighting swelled to a level I couldn't ignore when my apartment complex came into view. I wanted to ask if we could do something else together. But it was too early for dinner, and I had to take care of Paws. How could I ask him to wait around while I did my chores when he'd already sacrificed half his Sunday as a favor to me? And how could I silence that voice in my head telling me it was only a matter of time before this guy realized he was too good for me? Why couldn't I accept that he seemed interested without wondering how long it would last?

"Is your car at the church?" he asked.

"No, I walked."

"Okay." He turned into the complex. "Where should I drop you off?"

"Left here, then around the curve. That's my building," I said as I pointed.

He pulled into a parking space and came around to let me out. "Welcome home."

"Thanks," I said.

"Paws will be happy to see you."

"She might be confused about the timing. Later than church but earlier than work."

"You can explain it to her." He smiled only slightly and seemed to be stalling.

The reason hit me like a beam of light. A big, bright, glorious light. He wanted to kiss me. *Oh, Tracker.* I could call him by name in my head. *Go for it.*

"I suppose I should go home and do laundry or something else fun like that," he said. He looked hesitantly at his car.

"Thanks again for... I'm glad you came even though it turned out not to be anything I couldn't handle on my own. Long drives usually feel like wasted time but not... not today." It should be obvious that I wasn't rushing away either.

"It did turn out better than I thought it might. You really scared me this morning."

"I did?"

"I saw you come out on the phone and you sat down so fast I thought you fainted. I wasn't fast enough to catch you."

Had he tried? My heart beat faster at the thought. It wanted to be caught. *Please go for it.* He took a small step towards me and that button with the sideways X was right in front of me. I wasn't looking at it because it bothered me but because I was too nervous to look any higher. When I finally met his gaze, his intent was clear. And then it wasn't.

I watched his blue eyes dart to the ground and back several times as he became unsure. "I, uh... This is not... really a date so maybe I shouldn't be thinking... um... what I'm thinking?"

Oh, no. He was asking my permission. *Don't do that, Tracker. Don't ask me to admit how much I want this connection. I'm too scared to invite you closer. You have to come on your own.* "I, uh... I guess a trip to the hospital isn't... most people wouldn't call that a date." He could hear the doubt, right? *Tell me it counts. Or just kiss me. I won't push you away.*

"Okay." He stepped back and began tossing his keys between his hands. "I'll… I'll let you take care of your dog then."

In my mind I was throwing my arms around his neck and pulling him back for the kiss. I barely had the courage to picture it, but one of us had to be brave here. I offered what I could. "You know," I said, "you don't really have to have a dog to go to a dog park. If you wanted to stop by after work any day this week – unless it rains – Paws and I would be glad to see you."

"Yeah… maybe." His expression was thoughtful as he began to nod. Maybe he understood my offer of next time, of fighting caution and not indifference. "I'll keep an eye on the weather. Bye, Alexa."

He gave me a cheery wave as he drove away, and it patched up a little of the disappointment with hope. This would not be the last time I saw him. I could hold on to that thought.

Paws stood up and wagged her tail hard against the side of her crate as I entered.

"Hey, girl," I said. "Crazy day."

I let her out and watched her run around my legs before she shot into the bedroom. I talked to her as I changed into dog park clothes. "We had a bit of a scare this morning, but Dad's going to be fine. Tracker took me to see him and that's why I'm so late getting back from church. I saw Mike. I told you about him. He looks about the same and maybe he was only being nice, but he said he might call me to get together again. I probably won't be able to bring you though."

I put my foot on a chair to tie my shoe, and Paws began to pace excitedly. "Okay," I said, "I'm going to go ahead and say this out loud because… because you're a dog. I think something really good is happening with me and Tracker. He's… oh, let's just say I'm glad you like him too because we might be seeing a lot of him." *For a while.* I couldn't say that part out loud even if she was a dog.

I imagined that she was happy for me and not just jumping up and down because we were about to go outside.

"Alexa!"

My neighbor met me in the hall. "Hi, Deborah. Hi, Sampson." Her dog was already leashed and pulling her arm.

"Can you take Sampson today?" she said. "Please, please. I would owe you big time."

"All right." I took the leash from her and headed down the stairs. I took both dogs on a walk before I returned Sampson and went to the park with only Paws and my happy thoughts.

9

I had to work late on Monday because somebody did something stupid.

That's not true.

It was an honest mistake, and I only put in an extra hour so it's not like we were doing an all-nighter. I just got crabby when I felt like I was messing with Paws' schedule, and I'd done it two days in a row.

While we were at the park later, I got a text from Megan. I had sent her one the previous day to make sure someone had told her about Dad. Her reply: Mom left me a message. I called Dad today. Thanks.

Another baby step towards the relationship I wanted. If we could exchange polite texts throughout the year and catch-up at Christmas without me looking down my nose at her or her releasing an expletive-laced tirade at me, we will have reached my goal. I was probably only asking too much if I expected it to happen by the next Christmas.

I waited until we got home and Paws was settled before I called Tracker. I got voicemail and said, "Hi... um, it's Alexa. But you knew that. Paws and I missed you and Baby at the park today so I thought I'd check in. Talk to you later. Bye."

My dog had the softest ears. I think she knew I was disappointed to have missed him because she put her head under my hand as soon as I hung up the phone. After I gave Paws a good rubdown, I thought about trying to talk to my mom. But I didn't want to be on the phone if Tracker called me back. Mom could wait one more day. She wasn't calling me either.

I don't know if it was a nudge from God or a hint of how juvenile that sounded, but I reconsidered and dialed my mom. I gave myself a mental reminder to stay calm and positive and to keep it short.

"Alexa," she said, "I'm surprised to hear from you."

Ignoring that. "Paws and I are just hanging out. How are you?"

"Fine. I suppose you made it to the hospital yesterday?"

"Yeah. I'm glad it wasn't more serious. He didn't even look sick."

"I doubt Megan even knows what she missed."

We were on Megan already. It wasn't going to bother me. I would not let it bother me. "She knows, Mom. She told me she called him."

"You've been talking to Megan!?"

"No," I said. "I just got a short text that said she got your message and called Dad."

"She got *my* message and called her father? Is that what it takes? Do I need to be on my deathbed to talk to my children?"

I'm talking to you right now. Does that count for anything? I closed my eyes and held Paws a little tighter. "I'm sure she'll come around, Mom. Is there anything new with you?"

"I got a haircut this weekend, but I don't suppose that counts as new since it's the same haircut I've had for years."

"It looks nice on you though."

"Thanks. Megan got my hair and sometimes I think about growing it out like hers. I'm probably too old for long hair." Mom and Megan both had very straight red hair. I got a hint of their freckles but with dark hair like Dad.

"I don't think so. You can wear your hair any way you like."

"Maybe Megan has gotten hers cut."

Can we please talk about something else? Anything else? "I met a guy," I blurted.

"A guy? You mean someone you like?"

That's exactly what I mean. I like him so much I brought him up even though I was trying not to. "I don't know. He seems nice."

"Megan thought Chris was nice, too."

Yeah, and Megan also lied to Chris about being pregnant to get him to stick around after *he broke her arm. I am not my sister.* "I'll be careful, Mom."

"I know. It's a mother's job to worry though. What if

Megan is staying with someone like him right now?"

So what if she is? "So what if she is?" Drat. That one slipped out and I yelled it. There went the whole plan of staying calm and positive and I had mentioned Tracker for nothing.

"Alexa," Mom's voice was firm. "I know you don't mean that."

"No, you don't. You don't know anything about me. A guy could beat me senseless and you wouldn't know it because you never ask. You wouldn't even care."

"Alexa?" There was pain and confusion in that one word and I knew I'd gone too far. I hung up the phone and knocked it against my forehead. I didn't mean that. I didn't mean it and that made it even worse. My mother had her faults, but she loved me. I had never doubted that and I suggested otherwise only to hurt her.

Guilty tears made hot tracks down my checks. Paws sat up and licked one off my chin. "It's good that you don't understand me," I said to her. "I can say dumb things to you and be forgiven right away." I rubbed my hand down her side a few times. "But I still promise to try not to say anything mean to you."

I called my mom back and apologized. It didn't make me feel any better because she didn't answer. I knew I'd be apologizing to voicemail, and I knew that was the only reason I had the guts to call her back.

~~~~

I came home from work on Tuesday and faced the one, the zero, the two and the *four*. I just stared at those numbers. It was the stupidest thing to be upset over, and yet I felt the hold. I stared at the four and willed myself not to let it bother me. I was pretty much seething by the time I gave up and stuck my key in the lock.

Paws stood up and her swiftly wagging tail was a wonderful welcome. I dropped my bag and opened her crate. "Hi, girl. Did you miss me?"

She ran her usual circle around my legs and into the bedroom. I didn't immediately follow her. "I still haven't heard from Tracker," I called to her. "You were wondering about that, right?"

After a minute, her head appeared in the doorway and disappeared as soon as she saw me looking at her. I got the hint and went into the bedroom. "I know," I said. "You just want to get to the park quickly in case we might see him there." I began to change because I had a similar hope.

I filled up a water bottle to take with me. They had a fountain with a high nozzle for people and a low one for dogs. I had once seen a man letting his dog drink from the top one and held my thirst until I got home most days since. This was not most days. "Here's the thing, girl." I looked at Paws. "Today we hit triple digits for the first time this summer so there won't be much running around. We're going to stick to the shade as much as possible."

She yipped at me and jumped in a little circle. That probably meant she was agreeing to trust my judgment or that she wanted me to hurry so she'd have more time to run.

She was covered in fur so she'd figure out what hot meant even if my warning didn't do it for her. We were the only ones at the park when we arrived. Paws made a quick lap around the place before she joined me in the shade of a large tree. I tried to ignore the black car when I noticed it parking on the street. But I waved after the guy in the white baseball hat got out and started walking. I was going for casual, not oblivious. Though what I actually felt was closer to thrilled. Maybe I didn't hate baseball hats as much as I thought I did.

Tracker didn't have a dog with him, which meant he was there to see me. Only to see me. I was allowed to be happy about that. "I can't believe you're here," he said as he came through the gate.

"Why not? I'm the one with a dog."

His pace slowed. "I thought you weren't going to be upset about that."

"I'm not, I… I just wondered why you'd be surprised to find me at a dog park with my dog."

"Because it's ridiculously hot today. Don't you have limits?"

"Sure. You'll notice neither of us is running with a stick."
He was standing close enough that I was going to get a terrible

crick in my neck if I tried to talk to him like that. I nodded to the other end of my bench. "Do you want to sit with us?"

"Thanks." He adjusted his hat as he took the seat, rubbing the inside of it against his forehead before putting it back in place. He leaned forward with his elbows on his knees and didn't look any more comfortable than I felt.

I tried to relax myself with mundane thoughts like what I was going to have for dinner. What was I going to have for dinner? Could we talk about food? "Do you cook?" I asked him.

He laughed. "I try. I don't have the patience for recipes so I throw things in a pan and sometimes it's more edible than others."

"How do recipes require patience?"

"Maybe that's not the right word. I just never seem to have all the ingredients on hand and I don't want to run to the store so I'll leave things out or substitute. I'd plan ahead better – I think – if someone other than me might have to eat it."

"I don't really do recipes either but more because I'm, well, kind of a picky eater. But I don't want to waste anything so I make what I know I like over and over and don't need to look at a recipe for those." As soon as I finished talking, I realized that I'd focused on the wrong part of what he said. That part about eating with someone else might have been a hint.

"How picky is picky?" he asked. "You're not one of those people who says she likes say… spaghetti, but then will only eat it if it's made a very particular way?"

"I don't think so. Maybe it would be better to describe myself as not adventurous when it comes to food. I don't go out of my way to try new things, but I won't automatically turn up my nose at a new food. Especially if someone else makes it." Maybe I sucked at picking up hints, but I could drop them. Though I sort of thought we were past hinting. He showed up without a dog. I could look a little bit interested. "What are you doing this weekend?" I asked.

He squished his face into an adorably disgusted expression. "I promised my sister I'd help her move on Saturday. That's going to be fun."

"Is this the same sister who owns Baby?"

"No. This is Kayley. She's the one in the middle."

"And I assume church is on the schedule for Sunday?"

He nodded, watching Paws roll onto her back.

"Maybe we'll see each other at coffee and donuts again."

He kept nodding, but he didn't seem entirely convinced.

"You do like donuts, right?" I was so getting one this week.

"Of course I like donuts."

"Good. So you'll be there and I'll be there and we can, you know, talk… where there's air conditioning."

He cracked a smile and studied me for a moment. "Alexa… do you have plans for the rest of today?"

"Only that I have to call my mom again." I was dreading that, but I dreaded putting it off even more.

"I meant… uh, you two are talking again?"

"No." I sighed. "That's why I need to call her. We tried to talk yesterday and it ended badly. I said something I shouldn't have and… I think I'm really ready to repair things. I hate feeling this guilty."

"I'm sorry. Let me ask you a serious question. Would you rather feel guilty or wronged?"

"I'm not sure I know what you mean."

"Would you rather be the person who got hurt or the one who had to regret the hurting?"

"Neither," I said. "Obviously."

"I know. I meant if you had to choose."

"I'd choose neither."

"Yeah." Why was he starting to sound amused? "This is one of those for the sake of argument things."

"I hate arguments."

"And yet you seem to be looking for one."

Was I? I *was*. I was totally on the verge of getting upset over a hypothetical question. And Tracker calmly called me on it rather than getting upset right back. I definitely needed to keep this guy around. I'd start by answering his question. "Guilt is worse," I said. "I suppose I'd choose to be hurt if I had to choose."

"Well, now you're in trouble."

"Why?" *Are you going to hurt me?*

"You took so long to answer that I thought of something else to ask you. Was the chicken or the egg first?"

I'm sure that covering my face with my hand did nothing to hide the very unladylike snort.

"And no dinosaurs allowed." Tracker narrowed his eyes at me as though he knew I'd been thinking that and should feel ashamed. "We're talking chicken eggs here."

"Okay." I tried to look as though I was giving the question serious thought. "I guess the chicken might be the more biblical answer because God made the animals that went forth to multiply with, you know, eggs. But I like the idea of even the first animals starting as babies and baby chickens would need to come from eggs. I'm going to say the egg."

"I'm going to say that answer doesn't make a lot of sense."

It might not but I was sticking by it anyway. "It's a perfect answer. I have solved the riddle of the ages just like that."

Tracker laughed at me and said, "Now tell me what you like about your mom."

"My mom?" My stomach clenched at the thought of trying to have a conversation with her that did not involve my sister.

"Yeah," he said. "If you're hoping to have a positive chat with her, it might help to remind yourself of her good qualities."

"I thought you analyzed *numbers*?"

"I know that focusing on the wrong information won't give you a helpful answer." He shrugged. "And I'm curious."

"All right. My mom is… she's very organized and I've always admired that. Nothing ever got lost at our house and I've tried to copy some of her systems. She doesn't nag. Since I left home, she's never asked me if I remembered to do my taxes or set my clocks back or… It's like she trusts me to be a grownup. Though one thing I miss is that she used to tell the most awesome bedtime stories. That was one time Megan and I got along… when we were begging her to tell us another one about the time-traveling robot or the sarcastic talking turtle."

My stomach and every other part of me relaxed as I remembered and I no longer felt like I *should* talk to my mom. I felt like I wanted to. "Wow," I said. "I think you might be a genius."

Tracker shook his head with a modest smile. "I'm not a

genius. I'm just a guy with four older sisters. I know what it's like to have to remind myself why I like certain people."

"Tell *me* why you like them."

"My sisters?" He had this expression that said I might have just asked him to read the dictionary for fun, but I knew he liked his sisters. He helped them – with the dog and the moving and probably other things – like it was no big deal, and he had way too many fun stories not to enjoy his family just the way it was.

"Yeah, your sisters," I said. "Surely there were perks to growing up with all those females around."

"Nope." He moved his head slowly and seriously side to side. "Pure torture."

"I don't believe you. I bet you had fun getting them by…um…" Wow. I really had no idea what a little brother might do. My only brother was older and not exactly, not entirely… my brother. Not in a way that gave us any shared memories. "What was good about it?"

"A good thing about having four sisters? I'm drawing a blank here." I could see the corners of his mouth twitching.

"Okay. Tell me why it was so bad then."

"Oh, where do I begin?" Tracker sat back and waved his hands as he talked. "I don't need to mention the obvious bathroom problem, but I will anyway. Let's just say our house had two and a half baths and my parents wouldn't let us use theirs unless it was an emergency. But it wasn't even so much the time they spent in there but the stuff they left everywhere. Bottles and cords and I don't even know what all. I got like a tiny square inch of counter space to store a toothbrush and that was it. They outvoted me on everything so I never got to watch TV I wanted to watch or play the games I wanted to play and their friends were always so annoying. I asked to stay at my grandparents' house whenever anyone had a sleepover. Oh, this one girl was absolutely the worst."

He gave me a wide-eyed look that said I would not believe what he was about to say. "Cassie – she's about six years older than me – she had this friend in high school and every time she came over she'd say something like 'Cassie, your little brother is so cute' like I was some sort of puppy and like I didn't understand English because I was right there and…"

I couldn't even sit up. The laughter had exploded out of me before I could stop it. Tracker. A puppy. It was not funny. There was nothing wrong with his name and I didn't know why I couldn't stop myself from picturing a floppy-eared hound whenever I heard it or why the idea that someone else might have had a similar thought tickled me. But it did. "I'm sorry," I gasped. "It's not…"

"Are you going to tell me what's so funny?"

I shook my head.

His expression shifted from amusement to amusement mixed with concern, as if he wasn't sure he wanted to know why I was laughing.

"It's nothing." I pulled in the rest of the laugh with a very strong deep breath. I was done. I had to be done.

Paws sat up and cocked her head at me. Tracker gestured to her. "Even your dog wants to know what's funny."

"Nothing." I shook my head again and kept up the deliberately steady breathing. Tracker as a cute little puppy was not funny. It was a fine name for a person. No. Laughing.

Tracker turned away from me, and I thought he might let it go. But then he picked himself off the bench just enough to reposition himself much closer to me. He was so close his arm bumped my shoulder and the hair on his leg tickled my knee and something inside me stiffened in anticipation.

My hands were in my lap, holding a leash and flipping the handle around absently. A larger hand closed around that handle and rested against my hands before Tracker said, "*Please* tell me what's funny."

I couldn't tell him because nothing was funny. Every trace of humor had slipped from my face and right out of my head. He was threatening to take the leash away from me if I didn't tell him. My desperate imagination was sounding an alarm, trying to tell me that he was anchoring himself to lean over and kiss me. How could I want something so badly and still be afraid of it? "It was nothing," I repeated. "I just enjoyed you ranting about your sisters and… um…"

"I don't believe you."

I felt a gentle tug on the leash and I tightened my grip.

"Something specific set you off," Tracker said. "I want to know what it was."

I shook my head and felt another tug, not nearly firm enough to pull the leash from my hands. It was a test. If I let go he'd put space between us again.

"You looked guilty when you were laughing. In fact, you still look guilty."

"You're imagining things," I said. *Why did you give me time to figure it out? I don't want to chicken out.*

My fingers were loosening my hold on the leash even though I wanted to hang on. His hand pulled the leash and inched down it at the same time so that his finger stroked the back of my hand.

"I'll tell you," I said, "if… if you tell me that awesome band name you mentioned the other day."

His face broke into a surprised grin while he considered my offer. "No," he said. "I don't think that's a fair trade."

"Do you give up then?" *Or how about a different sort of trade? One that involves your mouth and my mouth and no words?*

He started to shake his head before his eyes met mine and he froze. I completely let go of the leash when he said, "I give up."

I don't know how I saw his eyes drop to my lips when mine were so intently focused on a point south of his eyes. But I saw it just the same. And I saw the bead of sweat making a line down the side of his face and I felt his hand cover mine and I noticed the way his head tilted to make sure the front of his hat wasn't going to knock against my forehead. My senses took in everything. Including, unfortunately, the high-pitched squeak of the gate that said we were no longer alone.

Tracker heard it, too. We both turned towards the woman and her dog entering the park. I recognized her even from the back, even before she unclipped the little terrier and yelled "Jack!" as he ran towards the water fountain.

Her shrill voice completely shattered the moment. Tracker let go of my hand, but he didn't slide back to the far end of the bench.

The woman yelled for her dog a couple more times and I rolled my eyes at Tracker. He gave me a commiserating look. "I suppose Paws has sucked up enough heat for one day anyway," I said.

Tracker nodded and used his shoulder to wipe that bit of sweat he had apparently not noticed earlier. I took a quick drink then called Paws to me. My voice came out a shade deeper than usual as I was making an effort not to sound like the Jack woman.

We walked out together, me and Paws and Tracker. I was trying to control my desire to ask when I could see him again. I didn't want to be clingy and besides, he was the guy. He was supposed to ask. It was because he was the guy and not because I was afraid he'd say no that I waited for him to say something.

That's not true.

Obviously.

"Alexa?" he said as we stopped at the crosswalk. I was going to go straight and his car was to the left. "Can I see you again?"

"Of course," I said. "Remember… coffee and donuts has air conditioning even if you can't make it to the park before then. But you can almost always find us at the park."

"Yeah…" He looked at the ground for a moment and nodded slowly. "Yeah. I'll see you soon." He waved as he left me with the weird feeling that I had given the wrong answer.

Paws and I crossed the street. I had sounded eager to see him. I gave options. He still had my phone number. Things were going well. It was only my ongoing fear that he was going to change his mind about liking me that made me worry. "Right, Paws?" I said to my dog.

She didn't even turn around. She walked with confidence. Lucky dog.

10

*I*t was too hot to cook. Or maybe I was too hot after spending time outside. Either way, I made myself a simple sandwich for dinner and gave Paws a few bites of crust. I never fed her from the table and since I was standing over the sink, I figured that didn't count. She was standing next to me with wide, hopeful eyes because she already knew it didn't count.

I was thinking about Tracker because… because I *liked* him. I had pretty much lost my head where he was concerned so of course I was thinking about him, thinking about how close he'd come – twice – to kissing me. That overshadowed any unsettled feeling I might have had an hour ago.

But I was also thinking about how he had suggested I remember my mom's good qualities because I was getting ready to call her. I gathered some fuzzy feelings about my mom and held them tight while I listened to her phone ringing.

She didn't answer, and I didn't leave a message. I waited five minutes then called again. Paws flipped over on my lap, and I gently rubbed my hand under her chin. I hung up on Mom's voicemail again. "Don't worry, girl," I said to Paws. "She'll answer sooner or later." Paws tucked her front legs comfortably against my side to show how little she minded anything that involved me sitting on the couch with her. I tried my mom a third time. Same result.

I waited longer – maybe fifteen minutes – on the off chance she was actually busy with something other than avoiding me.

"Alexa?" She sounded tired or possibly exasperated. "Is something wrong?"

"No. Sort of. I just… We need to talk."

"You already apologized and it's fine."

"It's not fine. I need to…" *I need to tell you that I feel ignored.*

"I know you're worried about Megan, too. I'll try to be more understanding when we talk about her."

I don't want to talk about Megan at all! "Thanks, Mom. I know you... I know you care what happens to me."

"Thank you for saying that. Do you want to tell me about that guy you mentioned?"

Yes. "Not yet. It's too early to know if it's going anywhere."

"Where did you meet him?"

"At the park. Paws introduced us."

I heard Mom laugh through the phone. We were having a conversation about me, and I made her laugh. "Megan always wanted a cat."

"I remember." So much for having a conversation that didn't include Megan. But I could handle a little reminiscing. We could talk about old times and change the subject to something else before anyone got upset. "Megan wanted a cat and I wanted a dog so we got neither."

"It worked because I didn't want to take care of either. I only wanted to take care of my girls."

"My dog knows I appreciate her more because I had to wait for her." I gave Paws a gentle squeeze as I mentioned her.

"I still want to take care of my girls. I wish Megan would let me. I went to see your father to find out what she said when she called him."

I bet Dad loved being in the middle of that. "Yeah?" That sounded like a wince instead of a curious question. Mom didn't appear to notice.

"I think he's hiding something from me. He said she only asked if he was okay and that was it but... I called her four times since. I just want to hear her voice saying she's okay."

"The line is open even if it's only one way. That signals hope." Monsignor Loy had told me that.

"What do you mean?"

"She hasn't blocked your number or told you to stop calling, right? She's not—"

"Can she do that?!"

Oh... I said the wrong thing. Mom had clearly not thought of that.

~ 73 ~

"Can she do that?!" she asked again with that high-pitched voice I knew would hear no reason.

Yes, Mom. Megan could do worse than not calling you back. "She's still listening to your messages, right? That's how she knew about Dad. I think—"

She cut me off again. "What are we going to do?"

"*I'm* going to live my life. Did I tell you I got a raise this month?"

"If Megan would stay in one job a little—"

"Can we not talk about that?" *I... don't... want... to... talk... about... Megan!*

Silence. It stretched on until I realized she was waiting for me. "Did you hear my question?" she said.

"Which question?"

"How long was Megan's longest job?"

"I don't remember."

"Oh, well. I think she'll find something she likes soon."

When she finds an employer who lets her come in hungover. "Maybe."

"What kind of attitude is that? I wish you'd be more supportive of your sister."

"I wish you'd be less supportive."

"Less enabling, right?" Mom's voice had a sneer in it. "Is that what you meant? I shouldn't give money to my child when she's near to living on the street?"

I only meant you don't have to tell me about it. "Help her all you want."

"Gee, thanks for your permission."

I don't know if it was her sarcasm or my frustration that made me hang up the phone. A moment of twisted logic convinced me that was better than screaming at her to stop talking about Megan.

Now I was right back where I was before I made the call. I threw my phone over my dog's head to the far end of the sofa. "Hey, girl. Do you have any advice for me?"

Paws rolled over. Her advice seemed to be a request for a tummy rub. I could do that. Why couldn't I control my anger though? I thought I wanted to talk to my mom. I was happy to hear her voice at first, but I just stopped thinking rationally every time I heard my sister's name.

"You keep working on me." I was talking to Paws, but I hoped God heard it, too.

~~~~

I arrived at the evening cycling class before the music came on. Only three bikes had riders, two women with their ears plugged and one woman reading a book. I was trying to make friends among people with different goals. But exercise was still good for me.

I claimed a bike in an empty row, leaving a space on either side of me for a chatty person to sit. I didn't want small talk, but I knew that's where anything had to start. Movement to my right caught my eye, and I turned to see who was going to be next to me. I was disappointed to discover it was the one person in the room who knew my name. At least, he better know my name. He had been my companion on the one date I'd had since college. The one official date.

"Hi, Marcus."

"Alexa." He jerked his head back in greeting. "Still single?"

"As far as you know."

"And still not giving me another chance?"

I smiled at his playful tone. "Still waiting for a good reason."

"Chemistry." He emphasized the word by sliding his eyes down and back up my body. Marcus made it plain that he dated in search of a good time and nothing else. While I tried to be coy, I definitely wanted everything else. He knew enough not to expect me to agree to another date. He only flirted with me because I was there. I only let him because, even though I wasn't proud of it, my ego liked the way he looked at me.

"Chemistry is the best you've got?" I said.

"How about... You're hot."

Marcus was clearly not an English major, though he was still in school. And just for the record, I did not know he was five years younger than me when I agreed to go out with him. It was a year ago. He was nineteen. If I had closer friends, they would certainly have made some not-very-funny cradle robbing jokes at my expense. I grimaced at his idea of a pick-up line. "You're not even trying to convince me to go out with you."

He smiled and began to pedal. "I'd try harder if you gave me some encouragement." He glanced my way with an expression that said I was welcome to come over and sit on his lap.

"I guess we're both out of luck," I said.

The music began to blare from the speakers as he nodded so I turned my attention to the front of the room where an instructor was about to encourage faster cycling. Forty-five minutes later I was the kind of hot that made me need to wipe sweat from my eyes. Marcus winked at me as he left, which I suppose meant something like see you next week.

A young woman whose stubby blond ponytail I had been watching for part of class waved to me as she turned around. "Hi," she said. "It's Alexa, right?"

"That's right." *You look familiar. Why can't I remember your name?*

"Libby," she said, pointing to herself.

"I think I would have come up with that in a minute. How are you?" I did remember her. We had talked about Marcus. I told her that he was younger than he looked. She said he was very cute but that she was happy with the great guy she was seeing anyway.

"Not bad. The heat this week is killing me though. I'm from Wisconsin."

"I don't know if anyone likes it this hot."

"Gives people something to talk about at least." She gestured to the door, and we began to walk out together. I noticed what appeared to be an engagement ring as she moved her hand.

"Is the ring new?" I asked.

She held her hand out to look at it. "Yeah. Only been engaged two weeks. I'm not used to wearing the ring yet. I wonder if I should take it off for class."

"Congratulations."

"Thanks."

"Have you set a date yet?"

"We're talking January or March." She paused with an intentional sigh. "Don't ask me what's wrong with February."

"I won't." *But maybe next time?*

"You're here every Wednesday, aren't you? Do you take any other classes here?"

"Just Wednesday."

"Okay. I'll see you next week." Libby bounded away from me as we stepped outside. A guy – presumably the new fiancé – was waiting for her in a gray pickup truck.

I walked to my car and leaned against it while my mind kept walking. It was going to be about two hundred degrees in there, and I wasn't in a hurry to experience that. Wisps of clouds were moving across the sky despite the still air at my level. It gave me a feeling of insignificance, as though the whole world was moving forward while I just stood there. It felt like a perfect time to pray. There was no one around so I took a chance on being the crazy person whispering by her car.

"God, you know I'm thinking about Tracker because I haven't stopped since I saw him yesterday. No one draws me out like he does. You know I've never told anyone else how I used to tease Megan about being smarter than her, and I didn't even think about not telling him. And when he flashes a grin there's that bottom tooth that's just a little crooked and… oh, I'm being sappy.

"Are you telling me this is right or…? If it's not going to work, if he's not the person I can share my life with… can you at least help me figure that out sooner rather than later? I know, I know… you can heal any wound. But right now it doesn't feel like that. It feels like I need this relationship. It feels like I need him to be something steady in my life. Like I can't get any more attached without…"

Wonderful. Now I was the crazy person whispering and crying in the parking lot. I opened the car door and drove my sauna home. In a show of mental fortitude, or stupidity, or following arbitrary dating rules or maybe I don't even know what… I did not call him that night. Something just told me to wait.

He called me on Thursday. We talked only a few minutes and he agreed to meet me at the park the next day after work. He mentioned that Friday could be a good day to do something without Paws after she was tired. This came across more like a theory than a firm plan. No one said the word date, but I was as excited as if we had.

11

*I*t was completely radical and yet so simple I could have kicked myself for not doing it sooner. I took Paws out before work Friday morning and when I came back up the stairs to face the one, the zero, the two and the four... I actually smiled.

I put Paws in her crate a few minutes early and took a screwdriver outside with me. I stood in front of my door and removed the one, the zero, the two and the horrible drama-seeking four and stuffed the numbers into my purse. I took them to a big home improvement store during my lunch hour and compared the available fonts. I found three numbers that matched my four. Paws might have sighed with relief right alongside me when I showed her our new and improved address that afternoon.

"It's perfect," I said. "Isn't it?"

She agreed with me.

I don't know if that's true or not, but she looked happy about something and I chose to believe it was our now fabulous address. Maybe she was even proud of me like I was a little proud of myself. I fixed it so I could let go. I finally wanted to let it go.

"Alexa!"

I tried to cover the fact that I had left my skin in a pile next to me as I turned to my neighbor. "Hi, Deborah."

"I don't suppose you could take Sampson today?" He was tugging on her arm, oblivious to the holdup. "You'd be doing me such a huge favor. I really mean it today."

"I don't know. I'm meeting someone at the park."

"Please, please, please."

"But you know Sampson needs the leash."

"He won't care if he's the only one tethered. Thank you soooo much." Deborah slipped back into her apartment. I was holding Sampson's leash without really accepting it.

"Fine," I said to myself. "I guess I'm taking Sampson. Come on, guys." It wasn't worth fighting over. I had the feeling that making Deborah take Sampson was likely to punish him as much if not more than her. And if walking an extra dog once a week or so was the price for having a friendly relationship with my neighbor, I would choose to walk the dog.

The dogs led me down the stairs, and we made a quick stop in the grass before I led them across the street. There were two familiar-looking people at the park, familiarly staring at their phones.

"Okay, Paws." I patted my dog as I unhooked her leash. "Try not to rub Sampson's nose in the fact that you get to run free."

She ran to a tree and grabbed a stick because that was what my dog did at the park. No leash meant grabbing sticks. She had a lot to rub Sampson's nose in. I did the best I could at chasing her and running Sampson around at the same time. Tracker arrived as I was getting out of breath.

"Dogsitting again?" he asked as he joined me.

"Yeah. And he's wearing me out. I'm going to have a seat." *And you're welcome to sit as close as last time.* I tipped my head to indicate that I wanted him to follow me. Then I sat on the nearest bench. I dropped Paws' leash next to me and wrapped the end of Sampson's leash on the arm of the bench.

Tracker sat on the other side of the leash. I kicked myself for putting it next to me without thinking that it might look as though I was trying not to let him sit too close and I couldn't move it now when he was already sitting and it didn't matter because I didn't want him to kiss me when other people were around even if they were probably too absorbed in tiny screens to notice. "So," I said, "are you going to complain about the heat today?"

"Are you kidding? It's like ten degrees cooler than the last time we were here so it practically feels…" He made a sound that I think meant he couldn't continue the charade of that sentence. "It's still too hot. But I won't complain."

"We'll just let the dogs stay a little longer anyway."

He lowered his chin in a nod. The front of his hat cast a shadow over his eyes – which I guess was the point of wearing a hat – but I was looking forward to seeing him without it on Sunday. Of course that was assuming he wanted to see me again after today. He was at the dog park without a dog again. And I still couldn't let myself believe this was going somewhere. Perhaps a kiss would help. Or some sort of contact. I dropped my hand to fiddle with the leash between us.

"Tell me about your job while the dogs are enjoying the grass," Tracker said.

"My job?"

"Yeah. Not the boring parts." The grin I liked flickered across his face. "But the people you work with and anything you particularly like or don't like."

"All right. I work for three... uh... When I started I was the secretary for two guys, Rick Miller and Rick Steinmack. I was just out of school and it felt weird – since they're both quite a bit older than me – to call them by their first names like they wanted and I convinced them that I needed to use titles and last names so as not to confuse anyone since they had the same first name. But now I mostly think of them as 'the Ricks' in my head. And then about a year ago I... There's another guy – not named Rick – who had a part-time secretary and when she left, they decided to save money by giving me her work rather than hiring somebody else."

"How did you feel about that?"

"Honestly, I didn't really have enough to do before so it's mostly good but now and then things do sort of pile up."

Tracker was fingering the leash between us now, too. "Do they at least seem to appreciate you?"

"I think so. Things are weird with me and one of the Ricks right now because of a non-work situation."

He tensed somewhat and his fingers stopped moving on the leash. "What kind of situation?"

He sounded protective, like when he threatened to make people be nice to me. It was sweet. "Oh, it's nothing... He's getting divorced, and I'm the only one who knows."

"Why... or uh, how...?"

"About a month ago, I was in his office sorting through some paperwork, and he was staring out the window just clearly not wanting to be at work. So I asked if something was wrong. He said, 'Last night my wife told me that we're getting divorced, and I didn't even know she wasn't happy.'"

"Wow." Tracker rubbed the back of his neck. "That sucks."

"I agree. They've been married eleven or twelve years I think and they have two kids. He seems nice at work but of course I don't really know him so there could be another side but it sure seemed to hit him out of the blue."

"Wow," Tracker said again. He was shaking his head. "You gotta give the guy a chance to make it right, especially if there's kids."

"Yeah..." *I love that you'd want to work on a relationship. I want to, too.* "But we don't really know the details and I don't want to. Anyway, after he told me he sort of apologized for telling me. He said he just had to tell someone and he knew I wouldn't spread it around the office. I haven't told anyone and that's what's so weird. People keep casually mentioning his wife with no idea it's a touchy subject and every time I get all tense and worried that it's about to come out and... it just makes me wish I didn't know."

"That does sound awkward." His fingertips loosely interlaced with mine. The touch was comforting and made the hairs on the back of my neck stand up at the same time.

"Oh, no," I said. It had nothing to do with Tracker, but I had to pull my hand away. I noticed that Sampson's leash had gone slack. At first I thought he had slipped the collar over his head. When I picked it up though, I could see that the buckle was broken. "Great. Sampson! Here, boy!"

I felt a little like the Jack woman because he completely ignored me.

"Sampson! Sampson!" Calling him was not going to work. There was no reason to panic as long as he was trapped by the park fence. I looked at Tracker. "I don't suppose you happen to have food on you?"

He laughed at my suggestion and didn't even bother to say he didn't. "I'll help," he said. "Maybe if I go that way and you go that way, we can corner him."

"All right." I walked casually towards Sampson from one side while Tracker approached from another. The dog was working his nose over a patch of brown grass. He saw Tracker at the last moment and lunged away from him and right past me.

Paws was trotting along next to me. She seemed to have recognized my call even though I didn't say her name. "You're a good girl," I told her and gave her a quick pat.

Then I stood with my hands on my hips to figure out what to do about Sampson. Maybe I could put Paws' collar on Sampson since she'd stay with me on the way home, except that we had to cross a street. I'd feel better if they were both tethered just in case. Paws would be lighter to carry. Of course I was getting ahead of myself. We needed to catch Sampson before I worried about how to get him home.

"Maybe, um…" I looked at Tracker. "I'll chase him and try to get him to run close enough to you that you can grab him."

Tracker shook his head. "*I'll* chase him."

The first part of the plan went fine. Tracker chased Sampson. But any time he got anywhere near me, he dodged me with way more agility than I had. I kept trying while I also tried to think of a better idea. Maybe I should run to my apartment to get a bag of treats. I could climb the fence to keep the gate closed.

One of the other people at the park was sort of smirking over the top of his phone. He seemed to have figured out that we were having trouble and found it amusing. But at least he wasn't making it worse, which was a possibility as another person had just arrived. "Don't let him out!" I called to the middle-aged man about to open the gate.

I really hope he didn't hear me – or at least didn't realize I was talking to him – because he opened the gate without even looking at Sampson. The yellow dog I was trying not to hate at the moment darted past the man's legs to a dangerous freedom.

"No!" I also screamed something that was not a word but more clearly expressed my frustration.

The man shrugged and said he was sorry with a trace of sincerity.

I looked at Tracker. "Stay with Paws for me?"

He nodded reluctantly. I think he wanted to chase Sampson for me, but he'd already been doing that for ten minutes and I was closer to the gate. I closed it and sprinted after Sampson.

The other time I chased him had been the first time I walked him for Deborah. I took both dogs to the park and let them run around. Since Paws was my only experience with dogs, I didn't know it might be hard to get one back on a leash until it was time to leave. Sampson wouldn't come to me and then someone let him out. Paws was already leashed so she ran after him with me, and I grabbed his collar only about a block and a half away.

I knew as I ran that I had been very lucky that first time. Now he was running like he'd been waiting for this chance of escape his whole life. I called his name a few times. I didn't expect it to help, but it made me feel like I was trying harder. He zigged through yards. I mostly stayed on the sidewalk, working only to keep him in sight until I could get closer.

He paused to mark a tree, and I mustered a bit more speed and hope. But he looked at me and then dashed into the street. We were on a quiet block, and there were no cars currently in sight. I ran on the street as well, thinking I'd be more visible to drivers than the dog. If I let him get hit, it would be the end of that friendly relationship with my neighbor and the end of me being able to live with myself for a while.

Sampson heard another dog barking and turned to run through a yard. I kept trying to follow, the distance between us shrinking and growing like he had me on the end of a yo-yo. There was a woman watching a couple of kids in her front yard. I yelled to her as we approached. "Can you grab him?"

She gave me a puzzled look and watched Sampson run right past her without moving a muscle. I was tempted to yell a sarcastic thank you, but I'm not sure I'd want to grab a strange dog either. I was just tired. And she did look apologetic as I passed her. I think she would have tried to help me if she'd had a few more seconds to think about it.

Sampson found a big tree that was worth a sniff. He circled it slowly with his nose in the grass at its base. I got to about ten feet from him and stopped with my hands on my knees, panting harder than he was. "Sampson," I pleaded between gasps, "come on, buddy. Please let me catch you."

He looked in my direction, but I don't think it was because I was talking to him. Then he sat down. He sat down!

I took a few cautious steps and reached into my pocket. My phone was the only thing in there, but he didn't know that. I hoped that if I pulled my hand out closed, he might think I had something in it for him. I held my hand teasingly in front of him, and he appeared interested.

I don't know what changed his mind. Maybe he realized he didn't smell anything. But he took off again, fast and towards the street. There was a car coming. I think my heart stopped, but my legs propelled me after him. I yelled his name as loud as I could even though I knew he wouldn't pay any attention. It was the only thing I could think to yell, and I was praying the person driving the car would hear me. I was praying that God would hear me.

Squealing tires pierced the air as the car braked hard. The sound startled Sampson, and he froze right in the middle of the street. I don't know if I'd had time to think about it whether or not I would have risked my life for someone else's dog. It didn't matter because I didn't think. I rushed into the street and tackled him. The front of the car wasn't more than two feet from my shoulder when it stopped. I was shaking when I stood with Sampson in my arms.

A woman jumped out of the driver's seat. "Why isn't that dog on a leash?!" she demanded.

"I'm sorry," I said. "His collar broke."

She forced herself to take a few calming breaths and then began to nod understandingly. "I'm sorry, too," she said. "You just... you scared me."

"Me, too."

"I'm so glad I didn't hit him." She sighed with her hand over her heart. "Or you."

"Me, too," I said again.

"Are you both okay?"

"Yeah. Thanks for stopping. We're fine."

"You sure?" She had left her door open and made a move to get back in the car.

I nodded. I'd also stopped shaking, and I think that helped convince her. "We're okay. Go on."

She returned to her place behind the wheel, and I got out of the street before she drove away.

An older gentleman poked his head out of the front door of the closest house. "Hey," he called. "I heard the shrieking tires. Is everything all right?"

"Yes," I told him. "No one got hurt."

He mumbled something that sounded like, "Thank the Lord," before he disappeared into his house again.

I closed my eyes briefly to follow his advice and then decided that I needed a plan. Sampson was letting me carry him at the moment, but he was big enough that I'd probably have to set him down if he put up a fuss. And with no collar to hold on to, I wasn't sure how that would work. I wasn't exactly lost, but I didn't know the most direct way back to the park and Sampson was going to get awfully heavy if he did let me carry him.

I walked to the nearest intersection and sat on the sidewalk at the corner. I tried to make Sampson as comfortable and secure in my lap as I could with one arm and then I took out my phone with my free hand and called Tracker.

"Hey! Did you catch him?" he asked as he answered.

"Finally."

"Where are you? Do you want me to come pick you up?"

"Oh, thank you. That's what I was going to ask."

"It's no problem. Paws and I are already enjoying the air conditioning in my car. Tell me where to find you."

I read the street names from the sign above me, and he said he would be there for us as soon as he could.

I stayed on the ground while I waited, petting Sampson and telling him in the most soothing tones possible what a stupid, stupid dog he was. I needed to voice my annoyance, but I also needed him to stay calm so he wouldn't try to run again.

Tracker stopped his car in front of us and reached across to push the passenger door open from the inside. He had a hand on Paws' leash, and she was in the backseat.

I struggled to get to my feet without losing Sampson, but I did it. I climbed into the car with the dog on my lap and I said, "Oh, I love you for doing this. I don't know how else I was going to get him back to—" The words pouring from my mouth crashed to a halt as I realized how I had begun the gushing. "I mean... Thank you... It's great that you were willing to pick us up." I tried to hide my red face behind Sampson while I reached over to close the door.

"I know what you meant." It sounded like he was smiling. Was it funny that I said I loved him? Would it be funny if I didn't only love that he rescued me?

Somehow, in the shifting of putting on a seatbelt, Sampson shifted in my lap so that one of his toenails gouged my leg just below my knee. I cried out and had to tell myself he didn't do it on purpose to keep from shoving him onto the floor.

"What happened?" Tracker asked. "Are you okay?"

"Yeah. He just scratched me." I examined my leg. The line was nearly three inches long, but it wasn't deep. It was only oozing blood.

"It looks like you chased him about three quarters of a mile."

"Is that all?"

"I meant to sound impressed."

"Maybe you did," I said. "But it felt a lot longer than that to me."

When we got to my apartment building, Tracker parked and said, "Wait there. I'm going to come around and take him from you."

I didn't argue. I was too tired to argue.

He opened my door and scooped the dog off my lap. "His leash and collar are by your feet," he said.

I hadn't noticed that. I'm not sure I would have realized I left them at the park until I got back upstairs to return the dog without them. I grabbed Sampson's things with one hand and got out holding Paws' leash in the other. "Come on, girl."

She jumped from the back to the front then out the door behind me.

Tracker nodded towards the building. "Lead the way," he said.

Paws actually led the way. She scampered up the stairs with me behind her and Tracker and Sampson behind me. I knocked on Deborah's door.

She opened it with obvious confusion. I explained before she could ask why a guy she didn't know was carrying her dog.

"The buckle came off Sampson's collar and we had to chase him all over the place."

"Oh, no! I am *so* sorry." She reached out to take Sampson but stopped herself. "Wait," she said. "Just wait one minute."

She ducked into her apartment, and I shrugged at Tracker, who was likely ready to be relieved of the dog. He smiled to indicate that he didn't mind one more minute.

Deborah came back and pushed something small and flat into my hand as she took Sampson's leash and broken collar and tossed them behind her into her apartment. "I know you won't let me pay you for walking him, but I was thinking about giving you that anyway and after today you have to take it. Someone gave it to me for Christmas, and I never shop there." She took her dog from Tracker as she spoke. "And thank you again for bringing him back. I still owe you."

My neighbor closed herself and her runaway dog into her apartment without any more discussion. I looked at the gift card in my hand. I didn't shop there either, but if I could get something for free I would consider it. Later.

There were more pressing matters at the moment. Like how was I going to transition from finding myself standing awkwardly outside my apartment with Tracker to being on a real honest-to-goodness date with him?

12

"Well…" I said slowly, thinking much faster. "This is where I live and… Do you want to come in while I feed Paws and then… We, um, we talked about maybe doing something for dinner together?" I think that was a question.

Tracker nodded and said, "Okay," like he was answering a question.

I tried to hold my hand steady while I unlocked the door. Unless that guy who came over to fix the sink in my bathroom that one time counted, it would be the first time in three years anyone had been in the apartment with me. My eyes scanned the place as we entered for anything embarrassing. It was fairly neat, except for the dog hair on the sofa. I put Paws' leash away and followed her to the kitchen side of the room. The sound of the faucet as I put water in her bowl seemed unusually loud. Her food rattled into the dish as well while no one said anything.

"Sit," I said to Paws.

She obeyed, and I set the dish in front of her. She dug in with her typical ravenous crunching while I stood and looked at the guy in my living room. He seemed taller inside and that struck me as a weird thought. He had taken off his hat. I didn't know if that was because we were inside or because he wanted something to twist between his hands.

I focused my attention on myself. Sampson's paws had wiped dirt all over the front of my shirt while I held him, my ponytail had come loose while I was running, I was sweaty all over and I was bleeding, too. This was not the way I wanted to remember the first time I invited Tracker into my home. Please don't let this be the only time.

He lifted an eyebrow as though waiting for some direction from me.

"I think we should go somewhere casual," I said, "but I still need to clean up because Sampson has left me a bit, um... disheveled."

He wrinkled his eyes at my word choice.

"A disaster?" I suggested.

"I was thinking of more positive adjectives."

Positive adjectives? There was something in his voice that made me want to turn up the air conditioning. A lot. "Disaster is not an adjective," I said.

He only smiled in a way that made me even more concerned about the thermostat situation. I had not planned on being this alone with him before certain boundaries were agreed upon.

"You sit anyway." I pointed to the sofa behind him. "And I'll change as fast as I can."

I locked my bedroom door because that felt proper and not because I thought I had anything to worry about. I hoped he understood that if he heard the click. I really did change as fast as I could and then moved to the bathroom to wash my face and that cut on my leg. I didn't have a bandage large enough to cover it, but it had mostly dried anyway. I ran a brush through my hair and left it down.

When I returned to the living room, Tracker was sitting on my sofa and Paws was cuddled up next to him. They looked so comfortable together I couldn't help smiling.

"She's allowed on the couch, right?" Tracker asked.

I nodded. The hair probably told him it wouldn't be a problem. "Are you hungry?"

"I guess we should go," he said, looking uncertainly at Paws as though he didn't want to disturb her so soon after she relaxed.

It really wasn't fair at all. I was already completely hooked so being nice to my dog was just overkill.

I put my phone and my keys into my bag and called Paws over to her crate. I knelt in front of it and mouthed the words, "I'll tell you everything when I get back."

She settled into her blanket, and I turned to find Tracker standing by my front door. His hand was on the knob, and I was ready to go. Finally. This was really a date.

He waited while I locked the door behind us. I noticed a small streak of dirt on the front of his shirt. "I guess Sampson got you, too," I said as my fingers brushed at the dirt. Partly I was showing him what I was talking about and partly I was trying to fix it. Then my hand froze because I realized that Tracker had come closer while I was touching him and I froze because I realized I was touching him. I looked into his eyes. *Kiss me quick. Do it before I remember.*

But I already knew it was too late. I remembered standing in a similar hallway with my last boyfriend, outside the tiny apartment where I lived the last two years of college. I knew something was wrong before he said anything, and I could still hear his words. "I don't think this will work because you don't know what a healthy relationship looks like."

He was wrong. It was true that I didn't have great examples in my life, but I had perfect examples of what not to do. I studied those examples, and I had been studying what God said about love. I wanted the kind of love that wasn't always easy, the kind that was permanent. But even though I knew he was wrong, the pain of him leaving me sliced from my memory and my hand flew from Tracker's chest. "Where do you want to eat?" I asked as I began moving towards the stairs.

"Uh…" He looked dazed and that was my fault. One second I was cleaning off the front of his shirt like we'd been together forever and the next I was running from him before he could run from me. I was literally walking, but the distance was no less meaningful.

If you ask me what just happened, I'll tell you. "Dinner," I said. "Where do you want to go for dinner?"

"How do you feel about The Sleepy Crab?"

"I don't know. I've never been there."

"You've never been to The Sleepy Crab?" Tracker had caught up to me, but his incredulous reaction stopped him in his tracks. "It's right around the corner from you."

"I believe I mentioned something about not being very adventurous when it comes to food."

"You did. But it's so close to you."

"I also…" *…had no one to go with me.* "I don't eat out very often."

"Good," he said. "Then it'll be a treat for both of us." Tracker pulled his keys out of his pocket when we got to the bottom of the stairs and tossed them between his hands. "Do you want to take your car this time?"

"You said it was close. Can we walk?"

"If you want to. I assumed you were tired from your unscheduled run."

"Unscheduled run?" That made me laugh. "Interesting way to describe the start of the evening."

He shrugged and dropped his keys. The faint crash on the sidewalk triggered a weird sound déjà vu. I felt as though I had stood right there and watched Tracker drop his keys before, but I knew I hadn't. I liked the feeling of familiarity even if I only imagined it.

"Where is this place?" I asked.

He returned the keys to his pocket with one hand and used the other to point the opposite direction of Sacred Heart. "That way. Then left and the strip mall is another left at the next block."

I nodded as we started to walk. "I pass that on my way to work, but I don't remember anything called The Sleepy Crab. Is it a small place?"

"It does have a small front, but it looks bigger inside. Now that I think about it, I haven't been there since last summer. We used to go there a lot when I was a kid."

"So you like seafood?"

His forehead crinkled before he nodded, but he wasn't answering my question. He was understanding it. "You're asking because it sounds like a seafood place?"

"It's not?"

"No," he said. "Common misconception. They have a big anchor out front and a whole nautical theme with pictures of boats and stuff, but the menu has a good variety."

"All right." My legs felt wobbly. I knew it wasn't from chasing Sampson, though I would likely feel that in the morning. The unsteady feeling came from walking next to this guy who was sending my hormones into overdrive, but with whom there was something undefined, or simply undeclared. I desperately wanted someone to say, "This is a date, right?" But Tracker didn't say anything like that, and I only asked a few questions about his job. I wanted to hear about it, but something about the conversation seemed... detached?

I don't know if that's the right word. I only knew that if either of us mentioned the weather before we got to the restaurant I was going to scream in frustration over the lack of progress in this relationship. On that long Sunday drive, we'd been talking like old friends. Why had this awkwardness returned?

"How adventurous would you say you are in general?" Tracker asked. We were about to round the corner to the strip mall.

"Not very."

"I propose we try a tiny adventure."

"What do you have in mind?"

"You say you've never been to The Sleepy Crab even though it's right here," he said. "Let's not have that be the only new business you visit today. Let's stop in every one of the places on the way no matter what kind of business it is."

"That's an adventure?"

"It could be." He tentatively flashed me a smile. "I don't remember what's here. I don't know what we're getting into either."

"Okay. I'm game." I shrugged at him. As far as adventures go, that sounded about my speed.

We came around to the first shop in the row and could see through the window that it was a hair salon. Tracker looked at me. "Well, your hair looks great and mine is..." He paused to slide a hand under his hat as though checking to see that his hair was where he left it. "It's short enough. Is there an excuse we can come up with for—?"

"They're closed," I said, pointing to a sign on the door.

Tracker read the hours from the sign. "Closed at five. I don't suppose Friday night is a popular time for haircuts."

"Not here anyway."

"Let's see what's next." Tracker urged me along and we came to a packing and shipping place. He pulled the door open for me, but I insisted he go in first.

A middle-aged woman with frizzy brown hair called to us from behind a counter. "What can I help you folks with?"

"Nothing yet," Tracker said. "Thank you though. We'd just like to look around for a minute."

She answered by drawing out the word okay into about five syllables, as though she'd never had anyone come in only to look around. She may not have ever had anyone come in to look around and that made me feel a little silly. I mashed my lips together to keep in the laugh. I didn't want to give away that I knew we were doing anything unusual.

Tracker led me to a large sign on the side wall that displayed shipping rates. He pointed to a box pictured in the middle. "I think this might be the best deal if... you know, we had anything to ship."

"Right. And if it fit in that size box."

He nodded seriously. I could see that he was also trying not to laugh but that he couldn't help crunching some of those numbers and revealing himself to be a bit of a math geek. I was happy working at a bank though so I wasn't about to call him on it.

"Now the envelope seems a bit pricey," I said, "because it wouldn't cost much more to go up a size and send something special with the letter. However, so much paperwork is emailed that there's something very... professional about anything that requires original documents."

"Like something with a seal," Tracker said, nodding. "My grandfather was a notary public, and he had this very cool tool for pressing a seal onto paper and I used to play with it. I liked to put seals on, like, old homework papers and stuff."

"Oh, yes. Old homework with a state or county seal would definitely need a nice protective envelope to mail. Or if it had a gold sticker. You can't email a gold sticker."

He laughed quietly as he threw a glance over his shoulder to where the frizzy-haired woman was still giving us the hairy eyeball. "Do you think that's enough research for now?"

"Yes," I said. "I'm sure this knowledge will come in handy."

We left in a hurry while I tried not to feel ridiculous and when Tracker politely thanked the woman for her time, she smiled as though they were sharing a secret. I was feeling more relaxed as we reached the next storefront. It was a gift shop. And it was also closed.

"What is with all these people not wanting to work on a Friday night?" Tracker joked as he began to peer in the window.

There were dim lights on inside that let us get a peek at the closest shelves. They were heavily packed with mostly useless knickknacks. Actually, a lot of it looked like things my mom might add to her décor. I should remember this place when Christmas got closer.

"Okay, let me ask you something." Tracker glanced at me then pointed through the window. I tried to follow his finger. "See right there," he asked, "that shelf with all the little glass animals?"

"I see it."

"Do you like those?"

The display had about twenty colorful translucent animals, each one small enough to fit in the palm of my hand. The light bouncing off them was a pretty sight, but Tracker was looking at me like this was not a simple yes or no question so I said, "I don't know what you're asking."

"Me neither," he said. Then he tried to explain. "I have to bring up the sisters again. You see, three of them are, I think, the normal... or regular amount of girly. They... They like things to match and admire something pretty sometimes and... But one of them, Cassie, she's like... I don't know. Her house is all... frilly. There's lace and bows everywhere and she's always changing it around and looking for useless decorations and for some reason I can just see her squealing over that sparkly alligator... or crocodile... or whatever that is."

"I get it," I said. *I sort of get it.* "You want to know if I'm squealing over the sparkly animals in my head."

"I think that's what I mean." He still looked confused.

"They are pretty but... well, you got a glimpse of my apartment."

"True. You did have that rainbow thing in the kitchen."

The rainbow music box he meant was pretty sparkly. "That was a gift from my mom."

"Okay," he said. "So no secret squealing?" He gave me a self-conscious version of the wink smile.

I shook my head. "I'm not a squealer. There are a lot of secret thoughts jumping around in my head right now, but none of them have to do with how pretty those animals are."

Tracker took a small step backward and eyed me with obvious concern over those secret thoughts. Since at the moment most of them had to do with how cute he looked trying to figure me out, he really had nothing to worry about.

"Let me ask *you* something," I said.

He nodded slowly.

"Which do you think would be a better name for a band… Sparkly Alligator or Sparkly Crocodile?"

"Hmm…" Tracker adopted a mock serious expression to give my question the consideration it deserved. "No contest I think. Sparkly Alligator has a much cooler ring to it."

"You're probably right."

"Let's see what's on the other side." Tracker motioned me to follow him to the window on the other side of the door. That section of the store was undeniably aimed at a different audience. The first window displayed fragile, decorative knickknacks while this side showed novelty or gag gifts. There were coffee mugs marked with cartoons and various sports teams. There was something that appeared to be the gift of slime – just what I knew I wanted – and a bottle opener that claimed to make rather unfortunate noises during use. A pyramid of can cozies had a black one on top that bore a picture of a shivering skeleton.

The idea of skeletons gave me a sudden, unwelcome thought. And a bit of a chill. I was afraid of Tracker losing interest in me. But what if there was something I didn't yet know about him that would make me want to untangle myself? And would I be able to do that when I already… already didn't want to?

Megan said it was judgmental of me to care about a guy's past. It felt like self-preservation. She was my sister whether I liked it or not, and I was going to love her whether I wanted to or not. But I would not welcome another person with ongoing struggles into my life with open arms. Megan was sober barely three months before she called me laughing uncontrollably about how wasted she was. As far as I knew, she hadn't tried again.

And what if Tracker had a kid? I hated the thought of my children growing up knowing someone who might resent them the way Mike and Sheila, especially Sheila, resented me.

"Something wrong?" Tracker was looking at me with a different sort of concern than a few moments ago. Apparently some of my secret thoughts were being betrayed by my face.

"I was… I…" *How do I ask if you're waiting to spring some sort of dark past or just… baggage on me?* "I, um… you don't have anything shocking that you're waiting for a good time or… um… any skeletons in your closet, do you?"

He laughed in surprise and then put his hand over his face to straighten it. "I'm sorry," he said. "That's not funny. I just… Well, I'm standing here trying to convince you that window shopping constitutes some sort of adventure so I don't know…" He stopped and fidgeted with his hat. "Trust me. You'd be more surprised by things I haven't done than anything I have. Let's see what's next." He waved me forward, away from the gift shop and away from what was evidently an uncomfortable subject for him.

I got the impression that wasn't because he was hiding something, but because he really didn't have anything to hide and that was somehow embarrassing. I suppose there were plenty of people who would make fun of a guy for being too innocent or having not sowed enough wild oats. It was fortunate for both of us that he wasn't trying to impress one of those people. But he was hoping to impress *me*, wasn't he?

He cared what I thought and a giddy and dubious sense of power came out of nowhere and made my mouth say, "Surprise me."

"What?"

"You said I'd be surprised by things you've never done. Try me."

"Alexa, I…" Tracker looked nervous. He took his hat off, rubbed both hands in his hair and then put it back on, having recovered a more playful air. "All right. I have never… ridden a motorcycle."

"I don't think that's terribly unusual. It doesn't surprise me."

"No? I've never… been arrested."

"Good. But that doesn't surprise me either."

"All right. Let me think." Tracker looked at the ground between us for a moment. "I never, uh…" His eyes came up slowly and my breath caught. He *really* cared what I thought. "I, uh… I've never been drunk."

"Not even a little bit?"

"No. I'm not sure I've ever even had more than one drink at a time."

I smiled at him to tell him that he'd won. "I am a little surprised."

"So that's enough for now?" His shoulders relaxed.

I'd be more surprised if you kissed me. Right now. You don't have to wait for goodnight.

"Alexa?"

Not going to happen? "Have we made it to the restaurant yet?"

He shook his head as he turned his attention back to our surroundings. "Looks like one more place before we get there. It's an eye doctor."

13

"It looks open," I said as I turned my back to the large window. There were plenty of lights on and people inside. "We don't have to go in, do we?"

"Of course we do. We already got off the hook twice with places that were closed."

"But... do you wear glasses?"

"I usually wear contacts."

"Me, too. And I already have an eye doctor."

"Is he as close as this place?" Tracker asked. He seemed determined to come up with a reason to go inside. I guess browsing glasses was not as good a cover for our game as reading about shipping rates.

"It's close to where I work and covered by my insurance and I have no problem with the doctor."

"Oh, wait." I could see the arrival of an idea on his face. "I have a totally legitimate reason for going in there. After you." He opened the door and held it for me.

One employee was helping an older woman make a choice from a wall of frames and another employee, a man with dark skin and a very shiny head, looked up at us from a desk with a computer. "Can I help you?" he said.

He seemed to be addressing me so I turned to Tracker to indicate that it was his fault we had come in.

Tracker approached the man and said, "If I brought in some broken glasses, would you still fix them for me if I got them somewhere else... and how much would you charge?"

"We'll adjust any glasses for free, including replacing screws or nose pads. If you mean broken as in snapped in half, you might be in the market for a new pair." The man smiled as though he'd made a joke, but he sounded serious so I didn't know which I misread.

Tracker nodded at him. "Good to know. I meant broken as in bent. I'll bring them in sometime. Thanks."

"Happy to help," the man said. Then he reached for a nearby phone, tucked it between his ear and his shoulder and began pushing buttons.

"How did you break your glasses?" I asked as we left.

"It was stupid. I forgot I was wearing them, and I knocked them off pulling a shirt over my head. I think they bounced off the bathroom sink on the way to the floor. Then I tried to bend them back into shape and made it worse. Now I save them for emergencies and I know I'd be annoyed if I actually had to wear them. It would be good to get around to fixing them."

My mind became a bit of a muddle as I tried to picture the brief story. I imagined it happening in my bathroom because I didn't know what his looked like. I was curious about how he looked wearing glasses, and I wanted to know whether he'd been taking a shirt off or putting it on. And that was something I really didn't need to be thinking about at all. It was a story about doing something stupid, and it made my face warm.

Back on the sidewalk, I saw a rusty anchor ahead of us and knew our adventure was coming to an end. My phone rang. I normally kept it on vibrate but had turned on the ringer before I went to the park in case Tracker called to say he was running late or in case he called to tell me anything before he joined me. I quickly pulled it from my bag. "Good timing," I said. "If it wasn't ringing now I would have forgotten to turn it off before we have dinner."

I don't know if Tracker saw that the screen said Dad or if he would have suggested it no matter what but he said, "I'll wait if you want to get that."

"Thanks. I'll be quick," I said as I answered. "Hi, Dad."

"Alexa?" he asked, as though anyone else would be answering my phone and calling him Dad.

"Yeah, it's me. I can only talk a minute. I'm with someone."

"On a Friday night? Is it a date?"

"No." *And you're welcome for not inviting follow-up questions.*

"I'm just calling because I talked to Mike, and he said he'd invited you to dinner next Saturday. Are you coming?"

"Yes." *And I'm sure Mike told you that, too.*

"That's great, honey. I'll be looking forward to seeing you there."

"Me, too," I said. "How are you feeling, Dad?"

"Still fine. I have a checkup next week."

"Good."

"How's that God thing working for you?"

"Same as always."

"All right," Dad said. "I'll let you go now, honey."

I silenced the phone as soon as I hung up and thanked Tracker again for letting me answer. I kept talking to him while I put the phone away, but I wasn't really looking at him because I couldn't seem to get the phone to go into the pocket where I kept it. "I like to answer when my dad calls because... well, if I don't he'll always ask me to call him back even though he doesn't have anything important to say and he only answers his phone about half the time so if we go through a whole round of phone tag to get to two minutes of how are you then it feels a little disappointing whereas if I just answer it feels... expected."

Tracker opened his mouth as I returned my eyes to him and then closed it before he said anything. I waited, but he seemed to shake off whatever he was going to say before he stepped forward to open the restaurant door for me. "Let's eat," he said.

"Good idea."

A sign that read The Sleepy Crab in red letters hung from the ceiling at the front of the lobby, and it made me want to duck even though I was sure it wasn't anywhere near my head. Tracker was about six inches taller than me, and he cleared the sign without a problem. I still felt as though I should squish my neck into my shoulders as I stood under it.

There was what appeared to be a hostess stand but no one behind it so I looked at Tracker to confirm that we should wait for someone to seat us. He was clearly waiting, which answered my first question, but his expression brought up a second question. Why did he seem to want to ask me something?

"Is something wrong?" I said.

"No. I was... um..." He turned to a very young man – boy was probably more accurate – who was wearing a shirt that said The Sleepy Crab.

"How many?" the kid asked.

"Two."

He picked up two menus and said, "This way, please."

If Tracker hadn't warned me, I would certainly have been expecting to sit down and order from a selection of fish. The walls were covered with pictures of boats, most of them very old-fashioned. The boats were old-fashioned. The picture frames had funky geometric patterns that didn't match the several hundred year old look of the boats.

The music playing was either a pirate song or a drinking song. Possibly both. I suspect there's overlap in those genres. The crab on the front of the menus looked anything but sleepy. His bugged out eyes and kicking feet seemed frozen in a perpetual dance or desperate attempt to escape capture. Probably not both.

"Is it just me," Tracker said, "or did the kid who seated us not look old enough to have a job?"

"It's not you. I'm feeling very grown-up all of a sudden. I don't know when I started thinking of teenagers as kids."

Tracker opened his menu, and I did the same. The first thing I noticed was macaroni and cheese on the adult menu. It claimed to be swimming in a sauce that was a mix of four cheeses, none of which had ever been reduced to a powder. I liked the sound of that. There was at least one option for anyone who had been talked into fish by the décor. A list of sandwiches ranged from an artery-clogging baconfest to something light with turkey and fancy mustard. I had a feeling I was going to like this place. Maybe Tracker would be willing to take me here again. Maybe regularly. Maybe this could be our place. How many times could we eat here before it stopped counting as adventurous?

"Do you play an instrument?"

I looked up at Tracker's sudden question. "No. Why?"

"I was just wondering what type of music we could play as Sparkly Alligator."

He was too good at making me laugh. "I did learn to play

the recorder a bit way back in… fourth grade. I doubt a plastic instrument would make music anyone would consider sparkly."

"Oh, we did that, too. So many kids squeaked them on purpose I'm not sure anyone would even call it music."

I looked back at the menu. Too many good choices.

"Did you make anything out of clay when you were in elementary school?"

"Pinch pots," I said while I continued to read about a salad described with mouth-watering words like crisp and tangy. We were slightly past my normal dinnertime, but I think the options would still have sounded good an hour ago.

"More than one?" Tracker asked.

"More than one what?" Perhaps I could not read and carry on a conversation at the same time. I hoped he could read the apology for not keeping up that I tried to put on my face.

"You said you made pinch pots. Plural. Did you make one every year?"

"No. I'm not sure which years we made them but I ended up with three. So did Megan. All six of them are on display at my mom's house on a shelf I made in sixth grade. Megan's shelf is holding the ceramic plates with handprint turkeys we painted in… I think it was third grade."

"Is your mom a saver?" he asked, trying to hide a disapproving tone. "I have a friend whose mom never threw away any of his stuff. She even has his baby clothes in boxes in the attic."

"My mom just has a thing for… trinkets." I pictured her windowsills lined with her mother's old perfume bottles and the mobile of souvenir buttons and the bookcase that had everything except books. "She buys keychains on vacations and likes commemorative things. She never saved school papers or old clothes. But she has the Christmas ornaments we made from a kit when we were very little and some random sun catchers and Megan was trying to sell jewelry for a while and Mom has one of her necklaces draped over a picture frame on her mantle."

He nodded and said, "Have you ever done anything crazy to win a bet?"

"Oh, are we doing the random question thing again?"

"Only if… if it doesn't bother you?" Tracker was leaning forward with his arms resting on the table between us. He sat back as he asked for my approval.

I love the random question thing. "I don't mind."

Someone showed up to take our order before I could answer the question though. I requested the macaroni and cheese because even when I was reading about the other options I knew I was going to get the macaroni.

"So?" Tracker raised his eyebrows at me after the waitress left.

"Anything crazy?" I repeated while I considered the question. "I don't think so. Not really."

"Not really? That sounds suspicious. Have you done anything close to crazy?"

"No. I was just thinking… Once in college I went to class dressed as a witch because someone bet me I wouldn't. But it was Halloween, and I was not the only one wearing a costume so it wasn't crazy."

"Maybe not. How many times have you been on a plane?"

"That's an easy one. None."

"Really? No family vacations or anything?"

"We usually didn't go very far, and Mom preferred to drive. My dad had a camper that we borrowed for a couple of trips and that was fun."

"Your mom took you camping in your dad's camper? He didn't go?"

"This was after my parents split. Dad liked to camp by himself."

Tracker started spinning his wrapped silverware like a slow-motion helicopter on the table. I watched it while he said, "Are you reading anything right now?"

"Not *right* now." I smiled teasingly.

"Thanks for that. It's good to know I'm not so boring that you need to pull out a book." He smiled just long enough for a rush of something very not boring to make my insides soft and warm. "But I think you know what I meant."

"I do," I said. "I'm working my way through *The Chronicles of Narnia.*"

"First time through?"

I nodded.

"Which book?"

"I'm nearing the end of *The Horse and His Boy*," I said as I attacked the paper on my straw with more force than necessary because of the minor embarrassment that came with the realization that I didn't know how long it or a glass of water had been sitting in front of me.

"Do you use a copier at work?"

"Sometimes."

"Have you ever accidentally copied the back of a paper?"

"No."

"What's your favorite...uh..." His face squirmed, and I could almost see the ideas being tossed aside as he tried to figure out what he wanted to ask.

"I think you're stuck now," I said. "There's no original way to finish that question."

"Leaf," he said.

"What?"

"Your favorite kind of leaf." Tracker's grin said he knew the question was lame, but that it was also original.

"I stand corrected," I said. "I have never before been asked to name my favorite leaf."

"Well?"

I tried to play along. "I'm not sure. There's so many nice ones."

Tracker kept grinning at my sarcasm.

"All right," I said. "Maple. But if you ask me to be more specific you're out of luck."

"Maple." He appeared to consider my choice. "That's a little common but still a solid pick. I approve."

"Do you bring a lunch to work or eat out?"

"Oh, now you think you get to ask me a question?" Tracker finally stopped spinning his silverware and put both his hands on top of it. I think one hand was telling the other to keep still.

"I've answered enough," I told him. "It's your turn."

"Okay. But that's a boring question."

"You get to ask me my favorite leaf, but what you do for lunch is too boring?"

"I think that's reasonable."

"Fine. Tell me something else you've never done."

"I have never gone skydiving," he said without missing a beat.

"That's hardly surprising."

"You didn't say it had to be anything surprising."

That was true.

"I have never written anything in wet cement."

"Also not too surprising."

His smug expression said it still was not a requirement, and I guess I wasn't trying to make it one. "I have never understood why the twelve is at the top on clocks."

"What are you talking about?"

"The top seems like where you start and shouldn't the one be first?"

I could feel myself shaking my head at him because I could tell this wasn't something that actually bothered Tracker. I knew about letting little things get to you, and he didn't. He was only trying to make me laugh.

"I'm not going to convince you that's wrong, huh?"

"No," I said. "Clocks are fine."

"All right. I have never tried to get away with driving backwards down a one-way street."

Now I was laughing. "Please don't tell me you're saying that because you know someone who did."

"It was my dad as a matter of fact."

"When was this?"

"About ten years ago. Maybe eleven."

"All right," I said. "Tell me the story."

"A family down the street had just bought a new couch, and they were giving us their old one. I went with my dad to help him get it into the truck. And then he decided that he didn't want to drive all the way around to get back to our house when it was only about five houses away. So he just backed up all the way to our house. I have no idea if that was legal, but he didn't get caught so..." He ended the quick story with a shrug as our food arrived.

I think he was hungry, too, because we were both quiet while we ate. Except that he mentioned he'd never gotten the macaroni and cheese, and that he planned to fix that on his next visit.

We did not get dessert, though I was tempted. I wasn't the least bit hungry after dinner, but dessert sounded like a way to prolong our time together. The quiet of the meal was a comfortable quiet. It wasn't the tense quiet of wondering what to say or that quiet I had at work when people were comfortably ignoring each other. I thought we were simply both in a happy moment.

There was some tension after the meal though. I insisted on paying. I pointed out how he'd driven me all the way to the hospital and he bought my lunch that day and I explained badly my need to contribute something to the relationship.

That's not true.

I said it very clearly, but maybe I shouldn't have used the word relationship or maybe it was something else that made Tracker uncomfortable. Something wasn't right, and that made me tense. As we began to walk back to my apartment, he answered my first few questions with, "Arrr," which lightened the mood again. Apparently, the pirate music had been getting to him as well.

He walked with his hands in his pockets. His demeanor seemed a little more aloof than the way there. I hoped he was only showing some nerves. I was certainly nervous. He'd almost kissed me after driving me around for hours. A Friday night dinner at a restaurant was about as stereotypical as you could get for a date. Surely he was thinking the same thing.

We stopped in front of his car, and he immediately began to toss his keys between his hands. "So how do you feel about The Sleepy Crab now that you've been there?"

"I think I like it. Everything except maybe the music anyway."

"I think the music didn't used to be so... I don't remember there being so much yo ho ho."

"I still had fun. Thanks for suggesting it."

"Yeah. I... I guess I might see you at church Sunday." He moved towards his car.

Where are you going? "Right," I said. "Donuts."

He nodded and waved before he drove away. I walked up

my stairs slowly. Paws stood to welcome me as I entered. I watched her tail swinging for a few moments longer than usual, and she gave a happy bark to spur me to action. When I opened her crate, she mashed her head against my legs then ran into the bedroom.

"We already did that," I called after her.

She poked her head out the door and dashed back into the room. When I took a seat on the sofa, she figured out I wasn't going to follow and she jumped up next to me.

"Don't worry, girl," I said as I stroked her ears. "You're not the only one who's confused."

She relaxed against me, ready to listen.

"Nothing happened tonight. I mean, we had a good time. I think we had a good time. We checked out the whole strip and we talked and laughed and... There were a few times when... I don't know. He just looked at me and I was sure there was something strong between us. But then he just left. No kiss. No let's do this again. No... I mean, he did mention church on Sunday and we'd already talked about that so maybe he's assuming we'll spend the day together because I'm kind of assuming that myself."

I kept petting Paws and turned on the TV. I wasn't paying much attention though. Had Tracker really changed his mind so suddenly about any romantic interest in me? Or had all those sparks flying around my apartment before we left been my imagination? The most confusing part was how unsatisfying a friendship would feel after I'd spent the last three years trying to make a good friend in Thompsonville.

Joyce was the closest I'd come to the goal. We'd taken RCIA classes together and she and I started our little coffee and donut group. But we saw each other only on Sundays. There was a limit to a friendship separated by sixty years.

I hadn't gotten beyond occasional lunches out with my coworkers and the gym was a dead end. I volunteered at the homeless shelter to focus less on myself but still hoped to strike up conversations with the other volunteers. With the rotating schedule I rarely saw even the regulars more often than every other month.

How could I possibly be thinking that I might have to stop

seeing Tracker if he offered only friendship? How could that be disappointing when it was so much more than I had now? Why couldn't all relationships be as simple as the one with my dog? She loved me because I fed her. She was loyal because I let her run around outside. And I would never let her down because I knew she loved me.

14

It rained on Saturday, and I took Paws to the dog park anyway. We had nothing else to do, and it was going to rain all day. We were the only ones there and by the time we left we were a soggy, muddy, dripping, happy mess.

But I was prepared. I had left towels on the carpet to make a path to the bathroom and all the supplies were handy for getting Paws cleaned up. She kept her head down and her eyes up in her most mournful expression while I talked through each step and tried to assure her that I was going as fast as I could. Then I gave myself a good scrubbing and threw all the towels into the wash.

I spent about an hour in the evening checking the weather for the next day and the movie listings and making a mental list of things I might want to do with Tracker on Sunday. It felt like I was prepping for an important test.

I put on my second favorite dress for church before I wondered if I might be doing it backwards. Perhaps I should have worn the third or fourth favorite the first time so I could work my way up. I convinced myself that was silly by thinking that his favorites were probably different than mine anyway. Then I stood in front of my mirror doubting whether *I* even liked the pink dress.

"The dress doesn't matter," I said. I might have been talking to my reflection, to my dog, or to God. I might have been talking to all three. "If things don't work out between us, it won't be because I chose the wrong dress. And I'm not going to let my gooey feelings get in the way of using my head." Then I closed my eyes and spoke only a prayer. "Is it possible to love someone you met two weeks ago? I'm trusting you to let me know if this isn't right."

I shut Paws in her crate and walked to Sacred Heart after *not* changing my dress. I didn't see Tracker at the mass or on my way to the parish hall. I turned my phone on and found that he'd texted me while it was off. It said: I'm sick. Sorry won't see you at church.

That was unfortunate. I tried to convince myself that it was more unfortunate for the person who was sick, but it was a hard sell. I wanted to see him. I kept thinking that he had better be *very* sick and that was not kind. I poured some coffee and walked towards the donuts to see if that would cheer me up.

Maria was near the donut line. I joined her as we looked between people at the choices. Someone had gotten the chocolate coated ones this time. Jackpot!

"They look so good, don't they?" Maria said.

I nodded. "Are you going to have one today?" *We can get them together. Come on, let's go!*

She shook her head sadly. "Sometimes I just want to look at them. I really can't afford the extra calories." She sighed and turned towards our table on the side.

I followed her. What else could I do? I couldn't eat a donut in front of her after that. Maybe I could grab one on the way out.

Maria sat next to her husband, who had brought two cups to the table. I sat between Linda and Suzy. "Good morning," I said to the table at large.

"How long before we get an extra person at this table?" Suzy asked me, her bright red lips in a sly smile.

"What do you mean?" I was not faking the innocence. I didn't understand her implication.

"We know you left us last week to talk to a certain young man. If things are working out between you two, you aren't allowed to abandon us. He'll have to join us." She curled both hands around her cup and laced together fingers with fiery red nails.

I guess I had been less than subtle when I fled the table at the sight of Tracker the previous Sunday. "I don't plan on abandoning anyone."

Joyce's cane hit the table on the other side of Suzy. She set her cup on the table and Antonio helped her settle into the chair while she fixed her eyes on me. "Tell us about this new man in your life, Alexa."

Had she heard what Suzy said or had she been waiting since last Sunday to accuse me of having a new man in my life? "There's not much to tell," I said. Since I honestly didn't know how things stood between me and Tracker at the moment, it was easier than I would have liked for me to play coy.

"Nonsense," Suzy said. "You rushed over to him awfully quick, and he looked delighted to see you, too."

Did he really?

Joyce patted the table in front of her as though she was giving my hand an encouraging pat from a distance. "Don't be shy with the details."

"I'm telling you all there's nothing to tell," I said. "I'm always eager to talk to a new acquaintance."

Linda snorted while Suzy said, "Where did you meet this new acquaintance?" Her last word oozed skepticism.

"At the dog park."

Antonio found this simple fact highly entertaining. Everyone at the table was either smirking or chuckling but as the only man, Antonio typically did his best not to draw attention to himself. His deep laugh was short but unchecked, and it made me feel I was missing something. Why was it funny that I met Tracker at the dog park? They didn't even know his name.

Maria, as usual, took the pressure off my confusion by changing the subject. "So Linda," she said. "News?"

"Oh, yes!" Linda put down the cup she was about to sip from. "I got the official announcement. She's due in December."

"A Christmas baby," Joyce said with a sigh. "That's wonderful."

After a round of congratulations and well wishes, we were back to talking about me. Suzy led the charge with, "Are we going to see your new friend this morning, Alexa?"

"That's an excellent question." A man's voice came from behind me. It was Monsignor Loy.

I turned enough to include him in my answer. "He's sick today."

"I'm sorry for him," the priest said. From the murmuring around me, Monsignor Loy might have been the only one sorry that he was sick as opposed to being sorry that he wasn't going to make an appearance. I was, unfortunately, not in a position to give anyone lessons on sympathy.

"You will, I trust, share with the young man my words of wisdom that he missed at mass this morning?"

The homily? Oh, no. Oh, no. I swear I had been listening. But in that moment I could not prove I had been listening. I couldn't remember a word he had said. I couldn't even remember the subject!

I tried to nod innocently. I wasn't lying. I was sure it would come back to me as soon as the priest wasn't looking at me.

Except for her donut avoidance, Maria was awesome. "I always enjoy the reading about the woman who touched Jesus' cloak," she said, coming to my rescue again. My nod became more convincing as parts of Monsignor Loy's reflection came back to me.

He put a hand lightly on Joyce's shoulder. "How are you feeling?"

"No more swelling," she said, moving her left wrist as though the movement was relevant. "I'm back to the usual complaints of someone my age."

The priest scanned his eyes around the table to see if anyone wanted to stop him then he moved on.

"Did you hurt yourself?" I asked Joyce.

"It's nothing," she said. She dismissed my concern with a slight wave of her hand before she mentioned a few things happening in her garden. I probably would have deflected questions about a minor injury myself, but it was surprisingly annoying to be on the other side.

Linda was also a gardener and had growth to share. Maria told us about the visit she and Antonio had with their daughter, who was considering a return to school. We even came back to talking about the gospel reading for a few minutes. I was not the first person to leave, which was unusual, but I followed Suzy by no more than five minutes.

~~~~

I pulled into my parking lot after work on Monday and walked up the steps to face the one, the zero, the two and the perfectly normal four. Something about those numbers made me feel powerful. I was taking some control in my life and especially of the anger I'd let infect even mundane objects. I followed Paws into the bedroom with my phone in my hand. I was going to call my mom, tell her I felt invisible in her life, and then never let Megan's share of the attention bother me again.

I dropped the phone on the bed a minute later. Talking to my mom was a good idea. Putting the conversation off one more day sounded like an even better idea.

"Ready for the park, girl?"

Paws yipped excitedly. Of course she was ready. I was the one who needed to change clothes. I pulled my dress over my head and switched it for a pink plaid shirt and shorts.

Paws and I walked across the street. Two guys and three dogs were already inside the fence. I didn't pay much attention to either of the guys, but I thought the one who looked up from his phone as I entered might have been the same man who'd opened the gate for Sampson on Friday. I thought this partly because he appeared to recognize me. He dropped his phone into his pocket and was beside me by the time I got Paws unhooked and told her to have fun.

"Hey," the man said, "you're the one whose dog got out the other day."

"Yes," I said. *The one whose dog you let out.*

"Did you catch him?"

"I did."

He nodded towards Paws with uncertainty. "That's not the same dog, is it?"

"No. She's mine." I also nodded towards her as she ran around me, no stick yet. "The other dog I was watching for a friend."

"That was nice of you."

I shrugged.

"Nice of you to run after him, too. My friends would just get a call if their dog ran off on me."

How nice of you. I reached down and gave my dog a pat as she ran another circle.

"I think you're here regularly," the man said, scratching the salt and pepper stubble on his chin.

"Yeah, we love it here."

"We? You mean you and your, um… dog?"

Who else would I mean? I just nodded at him.

"Where do you like to go when you're not at the park?"

"With Paws?" My dog was halfway across the park, but I think her ears twitched when I said her name.

"No, I meant…" He moved his hand between us. "Like if you wanted to do something with another person."

He was trying to ask me out. This guy who could not have been less than twenty years older than me… this guy whose stomach was hanging out the bottom of his shirt… this guy who I thought had been kind of inconsiderate about the whole Sampson thing and who hadn't even told me his name. This guy was asking me out. "I, um… I don't think I'm looking for anyone to do something with at the moment."

"Can't blame a guy for trying," he said with a shrug. Then he stuck his fingers in his mouth and whistled so shrilly that my teeth hurt.

His dog came running, and I worked to keep the wince off my face in case he'd be able to tell it wasn't entirely caused by his whistle.

I felt suddenly introspective as soon as he left.

That's not true.

Or not entirely true. I'd been introspecting about Tracker all day and all weekend, trying to figure out how our relationship got complicated. He'd almost kissed me when we were not on a date and didn't make any sort of move when we were. I couldn't figure that out. But my thoughts suddenly took a different turn. I paused in wishing things were simpler between us. The guy who'd just been here wanted to go out with me, and I did not want to go out with him. We hadn't spelled that out with the exact words, but the meaning was clear and it was very simple. Simple wasn't always good.

If Tracker had asked me out that first day I met him, I almost certainly would have turned him down. Mostly because of fear but also the fact that I'd thought him a little goofy. Now I knew I was wrong. Maybe I could put up with a period of complicated if we could get to a better kind of simple.

I pulled my phone out and texted him to ask if he was feeling better. When I didn't get a response, I thought of him possibly stuck in bed on a nice summer afternoon. I silently said a prayer for his health that had only a tiny bit to do with how much I wanted to see him. Then I tossed a stick and acted as though there was a chance I could beat Paws to it. She ran as though she believed it.

Tracker sent me a text around the time I was finishing my dinner. Better. Not 100% yet.

That gave me hope that he might show up at the dog park the next day. When he didn't, I got comfortable on the bench and tried to start some typed communication. I hoped that asking how he was feeling two days in a row showed concern and not impatient nagging.

He replied: I went to work today. I guess that means I beat the bug.

Me: Good for you.

Tracker: I know I shouldn't play hooky.

Me: I meant that you fought off the bug.

Tracker: Right. It was a valiant fight. You didn't get sick, did you?

Me: No. Did you have a lot of catchup at work?

Tracker: No. I'm valiant and efficient too.

Me: Any more positive adjectives you want to throw out?

Tracker: Sure. I'm responsible and imaginative and thoughtful and fun.

Tracker: And humble. ;)

Me: And funny.

Tracker: Thanks. You at the park?

Me: Of course. Paws says hi.

Tracker: If she could really talk, what would she be saying right now?

I looked up to see my dog looking back at me. Her ears were up and her head cocked to the side. I thought she was probably telling me to put away the phone and come play with her. My next text said: `I think she wants me to play with her.`

Tracker: `Not an unreasonable request.  Want to do something with me on Friday?`

I put both my arms up in silent celebration that he wanted to see me again even though my joy made the other people at the park look at me as though they questioned my sanity and even though Paws jumped up, thinking I was about to run after her. "Just a minute," I told her as I typed out: `Friday?  Why not join me here tomorrow?`

Friday felt like a long time away.

Tracker sent: `OK.  Go play with your dog.`

I took his advice and Paws' too as I ran circles around the park with her until I was thoroughly winded. We walked home slowly.

15

*C*omputer problems at work meant that I was bored for about two hours on Wednesday and behind the rest of the day. I came home and thought about calling my mom again. Then I didn't call her. Again. That was not good. The longer I put off talking to her the more agitated I was becoming at the idea. I was sure I was going to end up screaming at her again. And so I put it off again.

Deborah passed Sampson to me in the hallway with assurances that his new collar was very sturdy and that I had her undying gratitude for walking him. Despite what was so far a less than perfect day, my feet bounced on the steps as I made my way down them. Tracker beat me to the park. He was leaning on the fence near the gate as we approached, wearing a different hat.

Maybe I liked blue hats more than white ones. Maybe blue was a more flattering color on Tracker. Maybe I was finally associating baseball hats with this guy I liked instead of some degenerate at a party. Maybe after he dumped me I'd go back to hating hats. Of course he couldn't dump me if we were only friends and not even dating. I wanted some clarity on the subject. He smiled as I got close and that only clarified my own feelings. I'd fallen hard.

"Does this mean you've forgiven Sampson?" Tracker asked.

"Nothing to forgive," I said. "It's not his fault he doesn't know what's good for him."

"No, it's not his fault." Tracker looked at me when he said it and not at Sampson, which was odd. Even odder was the sensation that he wasn't talking about Sampson either. He blinked and said, "Are you going to let Paws run in the park?"

"I thought we'd just walk today... if that's all right with you?"

"Sure. Let me hold one." He grabbed Sampson's leash well below the handle while I worked my hand out of the loop. It felt as though Tracker was deliberately avoiding touching my hand.

I dove into analyzing possible meaning for the perceived avoidance. If we were becoming friends and everyone knew that, a casual touch would mean nothing. If Tracker wanted something more to develop, surely an excuse to touch me would be a good thing. The only explanation that made sense to me was that he was being friendly and knew I was getting the wrong idea. But that *didn't* make sense because he had seemed so obvious about having romantic intentions before. He'd even said he was being obvious! Why wasn't he being obvious anymore?

And did it have anything to do with the fact that I wasn't paying attention? I knew he'd just said something, but I didn't hear what it was. "I'm sorry," I said. "I was lost in my head. What did you just say?"

"I just asked if there was something on your mind."

You. Can I say that? Will you make an excuse to end this walk if I admit how much I'm thinking about you? I shrugged innocently at him. "I guess I'm used to solitary walks. Not that this isn't better."

"Paws probably doesn't ask you a bunch of annoying questions."

"I don't know anyone who does that. Wait. That's not true. There's someone at work who's kind of annoying. But no one around here," I waved my free hand in a circle past Tracker and the dogs, "asks too many questions."

He nodded and his smile said he understood, but he might have been concerned about making me eat my words because he didn't say anything. He simply walked quietly beside me for a minute.

"Sorry about the rain," I said.

He was very cute when he was confused even while I felt sort of funny about being the cause of that confusion.

"I mean on Saturday... when you were helping your sister move. That couldn't have been fun, and I hope it isn't why you got sick."

"Oh. No, I... I think I might have been coming down with something already on Saturday. Which likely made the rain less fun. But Kayley would have been annoying anyway. She kept changing her mind about what things she was okay with getting wet, and she kept changing her mind just in general. Like... put that there. No, it goes over there. Wait. Put it here. I don't care if it says kitchen, put it in the bedroom. Why is this box in the bedroom?" He rolled his eyes but seemed as amused by her indecision as I was by his impression of it. "Then at the new house, her husband backed the truck right into the yard to make unloading easier, and it got stuck in the mud and that, well... it was a mess."

"Paws and I were a mess on Saturday, too."

"You took her to the park in the rain?" Tracker sent me a playfully suspicious glance with his question. "I thought you were against her getting wet."

"I usually am. I made an exception because she was due for a bath anyway, and I thought I'd let her have a little fun first. I knew I'd get wet, but I planned to at least keep myself clean. Then I slipped in the wet grass maybe two seconds after we arrived and was muddier than she was. But the good part was then I didn't mind as much when it felt like she went out of her way to come stand by me when she wanted to shake herself off."

"You didn't mind as much?"

"At first," I said. "Then I didn't mind at all because we were having fun splashing around."

"I think I would rather have had your Saturday." Tracker looked as though he could picture me and my dog as a drenched and muddy pair. I might have been embarrassed if he didn't also sound sincere in his desire to join the picture.

"I'll have to invite you if... um, well... if there's ever another time when she needs a bath and we have warm rain on a weekend and I'm prepared to do extra laundry and..."

"I shouldn't be holding my breath for this invitation, should I?"

I tried to offer an apologetic expression. I would certainly align those stars if I could.

"Hey, can you swim?" he asked. The question seemed to pop out of his mouth the same moment it entered his head.

"A little. If you threw me into a pool, I would not immediately drown. But I would not be very graceful getting to the other side. I only had a few lessons when I was a kid. Can you swim?"

He sort of nodded and shook his head at the same time and said, "Not as well as I used to. I, uh… I was on the swim team when I was in high school, and I went to the pool near where I live yesterday evening on a whim. I felt really slow and now I'm a little sore today."

"You can probably blame both of those on having been sick recently."

"That's a good idea."

We had started walking away from the park in the opposite direction as the last time we walked together. This way had a path that veered off the sidewalk and circled back. I tried to steer Tracker and the dogs onto the path by stepping onto it as it came to my right. Tracker picked up on the plan immediately, but Sampson required a few explanatory tugs and Paws got overexcited and ran straight across the path to sniff a tree.

With the shifting involved in making the turn, Tracker and I changed sides of the sidewalk. I moved Paws' leash to my left hand to leave two free hands between us. I wanted the courage to take hold of his hand, but the bubble of confusion stopped me. I was afraid if I popped it I'd find out he didn't want what I wanted.

Because I was thinking about hands, I noticed that Tracker switched the leash he was holding from his right hand to his left, and then back. And then it looked as though he was going to switch again and settled for holding Sampson with his right hand and hooking his left thumb on the side of his pocket. "So you have a family thing on Saturday?" he asked.

I nodded stiffly as I thought about Mike and our dad and dinner.

"How are you feeling about that?"

I tried to exhale some of the tension. It was still three days away after all. "I guess I'm feeling excited about this chance to connect with some family but also... a lot of pressure."

"What kind of pressure?"

"I feel like... like this might be my last chance."

"How so?"

I saw concern in his eyes and didn't even consider holding back the details of an explanation. "I've gotten together with Mike a few times now and each time he's been the one who's made the invitation. First there was that time in college, then his wedding... then when I met him and his wife for dinner and now I'm going to his house. There was a year or more – three years this time – between each of those invitations and I never contacted him between any of those times and... I always wanted to and I always chickened out by convincing myself that he didn't really want me to be part of his life, that he only reached out occasionally out of some sense of duty. I know that's not fair to him because he's never given me that impression when we're together. Now it feels like... like things need to go well enough on Saturday for me to be comfortable calling him or else... or else he might give up on me."

Tracker was silent for a minute. He seemed to be thinking over what I said before he said, "How would you define well enough?"

"How would I what?" If he was trying to help, I didn't get it.

"I know you don't like arguing so that would be bad. But you don't have a history of arguing with Mike so what would be good?"

"Well..."

"And good."

I caught his tiny grin and his tinier joke. It was enough to make me smile as I said, "Not arguing. Not arguing would be good. And well... enough."

"But you didn't argue with him last time, right?"

"Right?"

"So what'll be different this time to make you want to call him?"

"I'm different," I said. *I'm more desperate for family.*

~ 122 ~

Tracker began to slowly shake his head, which I found annoying. He didn't know me three years ago. He had no idea whether I was different or not. He didn't dispute that though. He said, "I'm sorry if this sounds flippant, but my mom always said, 'It takes two to argue.' If that's really all you want it should be easy enough to avoid. Are you sure that's even why you're worried?"

This guy with the stupid baseball hat must have led a pretty soft life if he thought arguments were easy to avoid. I was about to tell him as much, in my nearly hysterical voice, when I realized that doing so would probably start an argument. And that keeping my mouth shut would prevent it. He was right. He was right, and it really ticked me off. Just not enough to start an argument. The whole concept was threatening to make my head explode. Then it did. It exploded around the understanding that going to Mike's house and simply not arguing would not be enough for me. "I don't want to feel like an outsider," I said.

"I wish that was something you had more control over."

"Thanks." I meant it. His sympathy helped. "I wish my family problems were as amusing as yours."

"You think our problems are amusing, and you haven't even heard about the library drama." His eyes widened in a way that said he'd be happy to tell me all about it if I cared to listen.

I couldn't resist. "Okay," I said. "Tell me about the library drama."

"You didn't say please."

"Come on," I said as my elbow nudged him in the ribs. Then I added, "Please."

He touched his side as though I might have actually hurt him. The touch was so light I knew I felt it more than he did. The feel of his shirt against my arm stayed with me long after the half-second contact. "All right," he said. "When they were much younger, two of my sisters, Brilynn and Kayley, were reading the same series of books. There was some confusion about who checked out which books and when and somehow Brilynn ended up paying a dollar fine for an overdue book that she insisted was Kayley's fault. There was a big fight and they both still bring it up every chance they get."

"Over a dollar?" I asked.

"Oh, yes. A dollar. If anyone says something about Kayley doing something, Brilynn will be like 'I don't know if she can handle that. She can't even return a library book on time.' And Kayley is just as bad. She looks for any excuse to point out how Brilynn 'can't even admit she was wrong about the library book.'"

"That's not something they're really still upset about, is it?" I could see the red that flashed in Megan's eyes whenever we talked about something that happened when we were kids.

"No." Tracker shook his head at the same time to emphasize that this was not the kind of fight that should worry me. "They only like to give each other a hard time," he said. "But every time it comes up, it makes the rest of us roll our eyes and wish they'd move on already."

"Is there anything that they give you a hard time about?"

Tracker said, "Of course not," with a tone that said I'd asked a ridiculous question. But I looked up to catch a shiftiness in his eyes as he thought of something, something he didn't want to tell me.

"Are you sure?" I asked.

He fought against a guilty smile. "Okay. It's possible that I may have done one or two dumb things in my life that certain family members trot out as entertaining stories. But people only laugh because the stories are... embellished."

I was pretty sure he didn't intend for me to believe that. "Embellished?"

"Yes." He nodded seriously and stopped walking. We'd made it around the loop back to the sidewalk, and I could see his car parked a few spaces down the street. He glanced that way. "You go to a gym on Wednesdays, right?"

"Yeah." I said it slowly, squashing any enthusiasm from the word, because I would skip the class if he gave me any hint of wanting to stay with me longer.

"I'll let you go then but first, um..." He put his teeth over his bottom lip while he reached a hand into his pocket. "Well... speaking of dumb things... I just thought that if you ever had a band you'd probably need like a mascot or something." When he opened his hand, that crystal alligator we'd seen through a window was resting on his palm. The sun twinkled against the many green facets of its body. I don't think that's what made me believe it was more beautiful than I remembered. Something deep inside me threatened to squeal.

I managed to turn that into the word, "Wow," before it escaped my lips. I moved to take it from him, and he closed his fingers over it.

"Just a minute," he said. "The tag on this thing said it was a crocodile, but if I give it to you, you have to promise you'll always think of it as an alligator anyway."

"Of course," I said. "The tag was clearly wrong."

He smiled and opened his hand again. "That's what I thought."

I took the alligator and held it up for a quick inspection before I slipped it into my pocket so I could take Sampson's leash. "Thank you. For the alligator and for walking with me."

"You're welcome." His hand came up and grabbed the front of his hat. He lifted it slightly, wiggled it and pulled it lower than before so that when he dipped his head and said, "Goodbye, Alexa," I couldn't see his eyes.

"Bye," I said. Then I watched him walk away with a heavy feeling I did not like. The alligator that was so sweet a moment ago suddenly felt like some sort of goodbye present. But it couldn't be a goodbye present. Nobody gave goodbye presents.

"Right, Paws?" I whispered to my dog. She turned her head at the sound of her name then let one ear slide back as though waiting for me to explain something. At a loss myself, I helplessly gestured her to cross the street towards our home. I dropped Sampson off and gave Paws her dinner before I left for my class at the gym.

16

*M*y phone rang as I was walking into the brightly lit room full of exercise bikes. I didn't answer because the music had started and there was no point in trying to have a conversation over it. I picked the first empty space and for once I didn't even look to see who was near me. For once my needs were physical and not social. I focused on the workout, pushing hard against all the stress in my life, pushing thoughts of Tracker leaving into the pedals. The class seemed shorter than usual, but my legs argued with that assessment as I tried to walk.

My mom had been the caller I missed, and she left me a message. My body stiffened before I even started to play it. I listened to the recording of my mother as I moved slowly towards the door. Her voice was forcing control from the first word. "Alexa. I thought you were only not calling, but now you're not answering my calls either? Is this because you've been talking to Mike? If you'd prefer to be part of your dad's other family I'd at least like a chance to state a case for flesh and blood."

I could feel the tension I'd worked off creeping back as I put the phone away. My mom had completely gone off the deep end, and I was drowning right along with her. On the sidewalk out front, I recognized the blond woman sitting with her legs crossed and her back against a pole.

"Hi, Libby," I said.

She used her hand to shield the sun from her eyes as she looked up at me. "Alexa. Hi. How are you?"

"I'm having kind of a lousy day as a matter of fact. How about you?"

"My day's been super," she said with obvious sarcasm. "We should have a club."

"Want to tell me about it?" *You don't have to.*

"These two people I work with got into a big fight this morning and one of them quit. It was ugly. And I just got a call from my boyfriend or, um… fiancé," a tiny smile leaked out as she made the correction, "and he got a flat tire on his way over here to get me. He has a spare, but he's never changed one before so I have a feeling I'm going to be stuck waiting for a while."

"I can give you a ride," I said.

"I don't want to bother you." Her hand closed on her bag at the same time, ready to pick it up and revealing that she was tempted by the offer.

"I really don't mind," I told her. "It can be my club dues."

She smiled and looked relieved as she stood and slung her bag over her shoulder. "Thank you. I appreciate this." As I began to lead her to my car she said, "So what's making your day so bad?"

"I've been seeing this guy, and I think he's losing interest in me, but I…" *I don't want to believe it.* "I'm just not sure."

"That sucks."

"Yeah. And my mom's… well, I hate to say it because she's my mom, but she's kind of a drama queen and we're having more trouble than usual getting along."

"I'm sorry," Libby said. "It's not the same thing, but I have a friend who's hard to get along with. She's just always looking for the negative in every situation. We don't live in the same state anymore, and the distance has been great for the relationship." She winked at me with a sympathetic smile.

Her story might not be as different as she thought. I was offered a job in my mom's neighborhood. I turned down the slightly higher salary to move to Thompsonville. I unlocked my car and opened the back door as she walked around to the passenger side. "You might want to keep your bag in front," I told her. "My backseat is full of dog hair."

She shook her head as she opened the back. "Dog hair doesn't bother me. It's just a gym bag."

We chatted as she gave me directions to her place. I learned how long she'd lived in Thompsonville and about the epic car repairs that had left her bumming rides the last two weeks. She thanked me again as she got out and said she'd save me a bike next Wednesday. Perhaps my efforts at the gym were finally paying off.

~~~~

I waited until Saturday to call my mom. My plan was to wait until Saturday to even think about calling my mom. I hoped that if I could put the tension between us out of my head for a few days I'd be nice and relaxed when I did talk to her.

Of course, the worst way to get a subject out of one's head was to try not to think about it. Tracker Briggs was the only person taking up more space in my brain than my mom. I hadn't heard from him, and she'd left me two more messages. I could only tackle one relationship crisis at a time so after I had breakfast and took Paws to the park and went to the grocery store and started some laundry and ran out of things I could do to put it off, I sat at my kitchen table and glared at my phone.

All I wanted was to have a brief conversation with my mom that did not end with me yelling at her. Monsignor Loy had said that I needed to remember that I could not change my mom, only how I responded to her. He said I had to know myself in order to do that. I knew I didn't want to yell at her. If I knew that though, why couldn't I stop it?

Out of nowhere – or so it seemed – I began to wonder why I was good at avoiding confrontations with my dad but not my mom. Maybe there was a reason I wanted to fight with her, or at least didn't try as hard to avoid it. I inherited my temper from her so our relationship had always had its occasional high-volume moments. It had only recently gotten out of hand. Only since Megan dropped out of the picture.

But Megan was still in the picture. That was the problem. Some part of me had expected my mom to shift her attention to me once my sister was no longer giving her new worries. Mom still didn't feel the need to worry about me, and I let that hurt me, rather than accept that I didn't want Megan's brand of attention anyway.

I wanted to tell her to stop talking about Megan, and I wanted to explain where my anger was coming from. But I hadn't brought myself to do that, and I began to wonder if that was because I'd known all along it wouldn't do any good. Mom would only take it as an accusation. Mom would use my issues to fuel her own anger. I could call her and continue to tell her the things she didn't think to ask. The only difference would be that I stopped expecting change. Worrying about Megan more didn't equate to loving her more, and it was time I believed what I always told myself.

She answered on the first ring.

"Hi, Mom. I'm sorry it's taken me a few days to call you back."

"Are you?" She sounded snippy, but I knew she would.

"Yes. I've just had a lot on my mind. Can you maybe… well, in the future… if I don't call for a few days or even a week… can you try to assume that means I have nothing new to report and not that I'm ignoring you?"

A sigh came through the phone. I think she was offended but trying to resign herself to the fact that I had called her eventually.

"So how you are doing?" I asked.

"Fine." Pause. "Nothing new to report here either. Megan still hates me."

Megan already? Instead of getting upset, I almost laughed at the predictability. "She'll come around, Mom."

"When?"

"I don't know. Let me ask you something. What do you think of the name Tracker?"

"What do I think of it?" She sounded confused but also distracted from thoughts of her other daughter. Just because I'd accepted Megan was going to be part of our conversation didn't mean she had to be all of it.

"Yeah," I said. "If you met a guy named Tracker, would you think his name was good or bad or…" …*that he had a dog's name.*

"I like it."

"Really?"

"Yes. I think I'd have to see the guy to know if it fit him. Are we talking about someone you know?"

"Uh… we were. But why don't you tell me about what TV shows you've been watching recently?"

She grumbled at me abruptly switching topics again, but TV felt safe to me, dispassionate and appropriate for avoiding tension. I ended the call while it was still short, and there was no yelling.

I tossed the phone aside and ruffled my dog's fur. She got riled up and ran off to get a rope for me to tug with her. I wasn't foolish enough to think fighting with my mom was all in the past. Megan would continue to be a source of stress for her and a sore spot with me. And sometimes Mom's drama would push my buttons. But I felt more peace over my half of the relationship than I had in some time.

I had another person causing me relationship anxiety though. So after I worked on my laundry and had some lunch and took Paws to the park again and gave up finding excuses to put it off, I sat at my kitchen table with my phone again. The phone was lying there with the screen dark while my mind lit up with pictures of Tracker. I saw him fiddling with his hat and tossing his keys between his hands. I remembered how he'd taken me to the hospital like it was nothing and made going to a new restaurant feel like an adventure and I came up with one more excuse not to make a call that might end the relationship. I didn't want to.

I'd live in hope as long as he'd let me. I texted him instead. Will I see you at coffee and donuts tomorrow?

No response. I chose to believe he was busy rather than avoiding me. I had a long drive before dinner anyway.

~~~~

Mike's house was larger than I expected. It had an intimidating stone front and a long driveway. I pulled up slowly, taking in the house, and parked behind a silver sports car I knew belonged to my dad. I checked my phone before getting out of the car and found that Tracker had replied at some point during my drive.

I'll be there. Good luck tonight.

Bolstered by the contact, I pushed my nerves aside and strode up to the front door like the invited guest that I was. Mike's wife answered the door.

"Alexa! I'm so glad you made it. Come in. You must feel like you've been in the car forever."

"Hi, Karen." Mike had insisted I shouldn't bring anything. He and Karen wanted to keep it casual. My hands felt noticeably empty as I walked into their house.

Mike was standing only a few feet behind his wife, holding a baby in one arm. The man resembled our dad with the exact same round nose. But I had never even seen a picture of our dad holding a baby and Mike looked very natural in the role. "Hi, Alexa," he said. "This is Baxter."

"Hi." I tried to include both of them. The baby turned his head against his father's shoulder but kept his eyes riveted on me as though I might make some sudden and terrifying movement.

"He just needs a bit to warm up to new people," Mike said, unnecessary apology tinting his voice.

I took a small step backwards to give the little one space. His brother apparently did not need the same warmup time. He ran up to me from somewhere nearby and yelled, "Hi!"

"Hello." I turned my attention to my small greeter. "You must be Bailey."

He nodded at me.

"How old are you?"

"Look what I have!" He held up his hand to show me a small blue car.

"Very nice," I said.

"It goes on the tracks." Bailey ran into the adjacent room where wooden train tracks looped around the floor. My dad was sitting in a recliner in that room, and I waved to him as Mike encouraged me to follow Bailey.

"Glad you made it, honey," my dad said. He didn't get up, and I stood awkwardly in front of him, wondering where I should sit.

Bailey suggested the carpet. He began tugging on my hand saying, "Play with me. Play with me."

"It's up to you," Karen said. "You can hang out with the guys or you can come into the kitchen with me."

Given that the kid's arms were about as big around as twigs, he was pulling me towards the floor with surprising force. "I guess I need to check out this train setup. Unless you want my help."

Karen insisted I'd be the most help distracting Bailey. I thought I could push a few cars on the tracks while I chatted with Mike and my dad. But Bailey's game was too demanding to multitask. He called me the conductor and wanted me to give his trains and cars jobs, which he finished as fast as I could think of them. It was just as well because the grown men were mostly talking golf, and since I didn't play I had nothing to contribute to their conversation.

The younger boy soon got impatient with being held, and Mike set him on the floor. Then he became a crawling Godzilla to the train village. Bailey's response was something like an air-raid siren, and I didn't know how to handle the chaos. Mike showed off his dad skills by calmly lifting Baxter from the center of the tracks. He planted himself on the floor as a barrier and set Baxter on the other side with some blocks he began to stack for the baby. Bailey replaced a few track pieces and stood up a sideways building while cajoling me into giving the black train a job.

My dad continued to drone on about the poor upkeep of a local course as though his grandchildren were not in the room. The topic eventually changed to Mike's job. He worked in the office of some factory, and I listened as he explained a new inventory policy. It was actually somewhat interesting in an it's-nice-to-have-some-idea-what-my-brother-does-for-a-living sort of way.

Karen announced that dinner was ready soon after that. Bailey picked up that blue car he'd shown me when I arrived and raced us all to the dining room. Karen offered me the seat next to her on one side of the table while Mike strapped Baxter into a high chair next to him on the other side. Bailey climbed onto a booster seat at one end of the table and placed his car on a napkin near his plate. There appeared to be an extra napkin for the purpose of reserving the parking space.

My dad was the last to sit, claiming the head of the table to my right. His eyes fell on me as he pulled his napkin from the table. Though he didn't say anything, I got the impression he was daring me to try to lead a prayer. I didn't normally do formal meal prayers because I ate most of my meals alone. I would simply close my eyes and spend a few seconds summoning some gratitude by picturing the people I saw lining up for meals at the shelter. Since I could do gratitude with my eyes open, there was no need to cause a scene. I picked up a bowl of baby carrots in front of me and put some on my plate with a small spoonful of dressing.

When I offered the bowl to my dad he said, "You don't do the God thing during meals then?"

"I… uh…" *I don't know what you want me to say.*

"Are you…" Karen's voice interrupted. "Are you a religious person?"

I nodded at her, feeling myself begin to blush.

"I'm sorry," she said. "I didn't know. We can wait if you need to pray."

I am praying. God, how do I do this gracefully? "No," I said. "This is your house. The only thanks I need to say right now are to you. Everything smells so good."

She nodded uncertainly and handed me a bowl of spaghetti. I think she relaxed when I took it. My dad was filling his plate with an expression that almost looked as though he was gloating. How mad would he be to know I was doing the God thing right under his nose? I was thanking God for giving me the words to smooth things over with Karen.

Mike was cutting some noodles in front of the baby. "I think you said Baxter has a birthday coming up," I said.

"Yep." Mike glanced up only for a moment. "He'll be a year old next Wednesday."

"I would have guessed him younger, but I've had so little experience with babies that I'm a poor judge."

"He looks younger because he's still a cue ball," Mike said as he gently ran his hand over his son's nearly bald head. The hair was light brown and was thin enough that if it had been blond, he would have looked completely bald.

"I'm afraid that's my fault," Karen said. "We seem to get hair late in my family."

"I hope for his sake that if he gets it late it'll stick around longer." Mike patted his own hair where it was thinning in back, despite the fact that he was only in his early thirties.

"I have hair," Bailey announced.

Mike laughed. "Thank you, Captain Obvious."

"The noodles look like hair." Bailey put down the fork he'd been struggling to use and picked up spaghetti with both hands.

It looked as though he was about to put those noodles on his head, and Karen must have sensed the same impulse. She put her hand on top of his and said, "The food stays on your plate." Her voice was firm but no louder than normal. I needed to keep trying to know her because if I ever had kids I wanted to model myself after a mom who didn't yell.

Bailey picked up his fork again. He gave me a mischievous look that said perhaps the two of us could find a way to get noodles in our hair when his mom wasn't around.

I tried to smile at him without agreeing to anything.

"Thanks for your patience with Bailey and his trains," Karen said to me. "You didn't have to play with him so long."

"I didn't mind. I haven't played with trains since... I don't even know. But it was still good dinner was ready when it was because I'm not sure how many more ideas I could have come up with."

Karen sighed. "I know. The kid can watch the same movie fifty times but needs imaginary boxes to contain something different for every delivery."

"It helps if you deliver people," Mike offered.

"People?" I crinkled my eyes at this suggestion.

"Yeah, like maintenance crews. You can have them fix something different each time and that opens a new category."

I nodded. That did make sense. But did it mean I might be invited back to play with trains again?

"Oh, you didn't get any bread." Karen was looking at my plate. "Would you like a roll?"

"Yes, please."

"Bailey. Your aunt would like a roll. Will you pass me the basket, please?"

He picked it up without batting an eye. I looked quickly to Mike, who appeared proud of his son's cooperation. My dad was unconcernedly spreading butter on his own roll. No one was going to correct her. Karen referred to me as her son's aunt and no one cared.

That's not true.

I cared. I was sitting at a table where I had a title and I cared so much.

17

I showed up for church early on Sunday. I wanted to sit
with Tracker and tried not to worry when I couldn't find
him. I sat alone in my usual place and felt more alone than
usual.

A strange buzz distracted me from looking for him as I
entered the hall. The murmuring revolved around the fact that
there were no donuts. No donuts! The first person I asked
didn't know what happened. Neither did the second. I poured
myself some coffee and looked around.

Maria was at our regular table. Antonio was a few people
behind me in the coffee line. Suzy and Linda were sitting, too.
No sign of Joyce yet, but she tended to move slowly. No sign of
Tracker, and he didn't have the same excuse.

I exhaled and tried to relax. He said he'd be here. I made
my way towards my regulars but spotted him just before I sat
down. He was outside where the double doors were open. He
might have just walked up and hadn't seen me yet. I made my
way towards him and didn't mind that Suzy noticed how my
path swerved. I only smiled back when she winked at me.

"Hi, Tracker." Oh my goodness. I finally called him by
name, and it didn't sound like I was calling it a dog's name like
I'd feared. It sounded like I was happy to see him. The scary
thing was that he didn't look happy to see me. Or maybe he did.
It was almost as if he was happy to see me, but he wasn't happy
about being happy. And that idea made so little sense I decided
to stop trying to interpret his expression and focus on what he
said.

"I heard someone forgot to pick up the donuts today."

"I'm really not liking whoever that is at the moment. I had
my heart set on something sweet this morning."

"I'm sorry." He looked it, and I got an idea.

"Hey! Do you want to go get some donuts?"

"What do you have in mind? I still need to go to church."

"Oh." Did he not plan on doing something with me after this? Maybe he only overslept or maybe... There were a few maybes I didn't want to think about. "Well, I think the place down the street has donuts. It's only like two blocks that way." I pointed. "We'd have time to get there and back."

He didn't agree to come with me in words, but by the way his body shifted in the direction I had pointed.

We began to walk while I asked, "What have you been up to this weekend?"

He shrugged. "So many fascinating things I don't even know where to begin."

I smiled as I bit down hard on the impulse to ask why he didn't call me if he was bored. I might not like his answer.

"How was your dinner yesterday?"

"Pretty good. I mean... parts of it were actually kind of boring, but that's... I'd take dull over drama any day."

He nodded quietly.

His silence scared me. I needed to keep talking. "And I talked to my mom without losing my temper. I think I'm finally ready for a new attitude with her. Instead of letting it bother me, I'm going to start counting how many words we can get into a conversation before my sister's name comes up."

Tracker smiled at me, but something was wrong. It was the sort of smile that didn't include the eyes. He said, "Glad your weekend is going well."

So far. "So far." *You have the power to make or break it.* "What would be fun today?" I asked.

"Um..." He was looking at the sidewalk.

"Maybe we should get small donuts to not fill up. Then I can take care of Paws while you go to church and then we can go somewhere for lunch."

"I... don't know."

"Would dinner be better? I thought since you're close for church and I don't know where you live that... Shouldn't I know where you live by now?" A tense laugh jumped from my throat. Why did I feel like panicking?

"It's only ten minutes from here."

"Okay. So what do you feel like doing later?"

He said what I was dreading even before I knew exactly what I was dreading. "I don't think I can do this."

I stopped walking and turned to him. "Do what?" I tried to casually ask for clarification even though I knew what he meant. I knew exactly what was happening. He was about to say he didn't want to see me anymore and I was about to go home and cry.

That's not true.

A stinging in my eyes said I wasn't even going to make it home.

"This?" he said, as though he was asking me what he meant.

"Okay. Bye then." I turned away because my eyes were about to start leaking and all I could think was that I needed to hurry home to Paws. I could cry in front of her.

"Alexa?" Tracker moved quickly to get around me and block my path. He saw what I was trying to hide. "Are you crying? Now I feel like dirt."

"It's not you," I said stupidly and tried to get past him.

"Wait." He shook his head as though something wasn't making sense. It was probably the fact that I was crying when we'd known each other for three weeks. "Forget I said anything," he said. "Let's, um... let's... We haven't even gotten the donuts."

I guilted him into spending time with me. That was so far from a victory that my tears began to harden into a safer emotion. "No. You don't have to... Don't worry about it."

"Alexa, I don't..." He looked helpless and didn't try to stop me from walking away.

I spun back to face him after a few steps. "I don't understand you!" I was yelling. The anger pushed all the hurt aside and took control of my mouth. "Why did you do this? Why did you try so hard? It feels like you went out of your way to make me like you just so you could walk away."

"I never... I wasn't trying to make a *friend*."

"I know!" Or I thought I knew. I felt a growing confusion about something, something I was too upset to understand.

"You know?" Tracker still seemed perfectly calm. Flustered, yes, but calm at the same time. Who would have thought that possible? "Do you know that I borrowed my sister's dog just so I could meet you?"

"You said you were watching the dog because your sister had a baby."

"I was. Sort of. She did have a baby, and I told her that was why I wanted to watch the dog for a while but..." He ran his hand through his hair as though he was trying to make it lie down. It was already fine. Maybe he missed the hat I didn't miss.

"I saw you," he said. "I saw you at coffee and donuts a few times, but you were leaving about the same time I got there because I guess you went to the early mass. So I went to the 8:30 and still didn't get a chance to talk to you because you were sitting with those people who all seemed to know each other and I didn't want to interrupt. Then you left before I... After you left I asked about you. One of the women you were with told me you were always in a hurry to get your dog to the park across the street so I got an idea." He flashed a nervous grin. "And a dog."

"Why are you telling me that? Just so you can point out exactly when you changed your mind?"

"I didn't change my mind. I'd come up with a thousand more excuses to talk to you if I thought I had a chance here. But I can't... If you're not interested in more than friendship then I can't keep trying. I like you way too much to settle."

I heard what he said. I heard it, and it should have made me very happy but for some reason I couldn't explain I still wanted to yell at him. "What makes you think I'm not interested!?"

"Wait a minute." He looked confused.

If I could only settle down for a moment maybe I could figure out what was happening. But I was too angry. "Tell me why you think I'm not interested," I demanded.

"Are you saying...?" He hesitated and I forcefully pulled my hands up to my hips. He already put his cards on the table. Telling me what he thought I was holding should be easier.

"Go ahead," I said. "Tell me."

"Because you keep suggesting we meet at the dog park or at church or… It feels like you're trying to avoid anything that looks like a real date."

"What was last Friday?"

"Well, I thought… or hoped… but…" Tracker gave an apologetic shrug. "I wasn't trying to eavesdrop, but either your phone is loud or your dad is because I heard your conversation with him outside the restaurant. I heard what he asked you when you said you were with someone. And you said no."

"I said no because I was talking to my dad." I was trying not to call him an idiot for paying attention to something I said to my dad, but I'm pretty sure my tone used the word. "Don't you have enough sense to know that didn't mean anything? I don't talk about… I don't intend to tell my dad I'm dating anyone until I need him to walk me down the aisle. And even then I don't know if he'd agree to set foot in a church. But that's a whole other issue."

"You could have said maybe or I don't know yet or even I don't want to talk about that now. You didn't have to be so definitive." Was it my imagination or was Tracker trying really hard not to laugh at me?

"I was talking to my dad. It still didn't mean anything. And it's not funny."

"You said it to me, too."

"Because you were eavesdropping?"

"No. Before. We got back from that long drive and… you know what almost… that I almost…" He bit back a smile and lost his composure to embarrassment. It helped me to let go of the anger and admit that it felt good to have a meaningful conversation. Even though it was awkward, we were really talking. Finally, he spit out the words, "You said it wasn't a date."

"I said…" What were my exact words? "I think I said most people wouldn't call it a date."

"Yeah. And most people would interpret that to mean I don't like you like that, but I'm trying to be nice."

It was only a very small laugh. "In what universe does it mean that?"

Tracker laughed, too, before he defended himself. "That is not a stretch. But tell me what you... What did it mean in your universe?"

"It meant... I don't know."

"You don't know what it meant or it meant I don't know?" His eyes searched my face for meaning. It was clear he thought I did know.

I took myself back to that moment of the first time I thought he might kiss me and remembered the hope and the fear and everything else I was suddenly willing to share with him. "It meant I'm scared. It meant don't hurt me. It meant I want you to kiss me so bad I could scream, but I can't say that because *you're* the one who suggested this wasn't a date."

Tracker's eyebrows lifted as a smile spread slowly over his face, his entire face. And then it disappeared as a disturbing thought must have snuck up on him. He put both hands in his hair, digging his fingers in as though he was trying to pull some of it out. "Oh, I don't believe this."

"What is it?"

"You're telling me that *I* screwed this up." He looked at me in disbelief.

I wasn't trying to blame him. "That's not... I didn't mean to... um..."

"You just said I should have kissed you and kept my mouth shut." He shifted uncomfortably as soon as the words left his mouth.

I thought about what he'd said and realized why he looked embarrassed. My hand covered my mouth to stifle the giggles. I was not a giggling sort of person. I still couldn't help it. I wanted to say he didn't have to do both, but there was no need for both of us to be blushing. I forced myself to be serious.

"Alexa?" He reached out and took my hand in his. "The bottom line here I think is that you *are* willing to give me a shot. Am I right?"

"You are the one who tried to end this."

He rolled his eyes, but I don't think it was aimed at me. "Okay. We've confirmed that I am an idiot. Can we confirm that you're going to give me a shot anyway? All right, Alexa?"

"All right…" *But I still can't say your name.* I said it once. Why couldn't I say it again?

"Is my name that bad?"

Now he could read my mind? I shook my head. "It's really not. I just…" If we were going to work out, I had to be able to tell him anything. "I don't want to offend you. Tracker just… it sounds like a dog's name to me."

He shrugged. "I can see that. Do you think you'll get used to it?"

Are you going to give me time to get used to it? "I'll try."

"Good." It seemed as though he stopped himself from saying something else. He kept looking at me, and I wondered if he was waiting for me to call him by name to prove I was getting used to it. But then it dawned on me that he was taking his own advice. At least part of it. He was going to kiss me without asking first. And then he did.

When other guys had kissed me – and there hadn't been that many – it had always felt like a statement. It felt like they were saying *I like you* or maybe only *I want to kiss you*. But Tracker's kiss felt like a question. It felt like he was asking me to let him close, begging me to let him be a permanent bright spot in my life.

It was too soon to know if it would be permanent, but I kissed him back with assurance that I was hoping for the same thing. And I let myself trust in that hope. I kissed him without worrying about where we were headed and without thinking about the future at all.

That's not true.

A tiny part of my brain did wonder if I was ever going to get a donut.

~~ The End ~~

Also by Amanda Hamm

Weathering Evan

Meet Cute: 5 Romantic Short Stories

The 4th Floor Lounge

Andrew's Key (Stories From Hartford #1)

Jealousy & Yams (Stories From Hartford #2)

Collecting Zebras (Stories From Hartford #3)

The Christmas Project (Stories From Hartford #4)

Sofie Waits (A Coffee and Donuts Book) **Expected Nov. 2015**

www.ingramcontent.com/pod-product-compliance
Lightning Source LLC
Chambersburg PA
CBHW030616130626
46552CB00002B/586